bling addiction

Also by Kylie Adams

Cruel Summer,
Book 1 in the Fast Girls, Hot Boys series

Available from MTV Books

bling addiction
kylie adams

a
fast girls,
hot boys
novel

POCKET BOOKS   MTV BOOKS

New York   London   Toronto   Sydney

POCKET BOOKS, a division of Simon & Schuster, Inc.
1230 Avenue of the Americas, New York, NY 10020

ISBN-13: 978-1-4165-2041-2
ISBN-10:   1-4165-2041-4

This MTV Books/Pocket Books trade paperback edition August 2006

10 9 8 7 6 5 4 3 2 1

For information regarding special discounts for bulk purchases,
please contact Simon & Schuster Special Sales at 1-800-456-6798 or
business@simonandschuster.com

For Michael Kirby—
great friend, maddening rival,
nuclear-level smart-ass, and inspiration
for the Max Biaggi Jr. character.

He gone make it into a Benz
out of that Datsun
He got that ambition baby look in his eyes
This week he moppin' floorz
next week it's the fries

—Kanye West
"Gold Digger"

bling addiction

From: Bijou

I watched someone die tonight.

10:08 pm 5/26/06

prologue

L ife changes fast."

Bijou Ross, valedictorian, Class of 2006, paused the moment her words hit the air. And it wasn't because the soon-to-be-published writer and (if the hyperbole of *Entertainment Weekly* was to be believed) the "voice of the next generation" had just uttered what most certainly could be considered a hopeless cliché.

Right now it was the silence of the crowd affecting her, not the pedestrian turn of phrase. She felt her heartbeat pick up speed. Here, in the auditorium of the Miami Academy for Creative and Performing Arts, it was so eerily quiet that the lack of sound seemed . . . *loud*.

With a commanding control of herself that she didn't necessarily feel, Bijou continued. "Last night we went to a party, and life as we knew it ended there. After I got home, I didn't sleep. For the longest time I stared at the ceiling, half believing that if I just wished hard enough, I could change the outcome . . . and that our friend would still be alive today."

Bijou hesitated again, peering out into the audience. On the somber faces before her, she could see the grief, pick up on the erosion of mortal innocence, and practically make out the what-if links of causation churning in their self-absorbed minds.

What if I'd arrived at the party ten minutes earlier? Would things have turned out differently? What if I'd been hanging out near the bar instead of the game room downstairs? Would that have made *me* the one that the paramedics carried away?

But Bijou was struck most of all by the palpable absence of nothing-will-ever-happen-to-me arrogance, that maddening quality every seventeen-year-old seemed to possess, some more than others.

Bijou took in a deep, emotional breath, shutting her eyes as the image tattooed itself onto her brain, cutting into her psyche so vividly that she gripped the lectern to steady herself. It was a vision of someone just like her—same age, similar dreams—coughing up blood, bleeding out from the chest, losing the live-or-die battle within minutes of the explosive gunshot.

With heartbreaking sadness, she went on. "None of us possesses the power to reverse the tragedy of life. And there is no making sense out of what is senseless. The violent crime that we witnessed is a random act in the same way that a car accident, an airplane crash, or a terrorist attack might be. In one moment life can be normal, and in the next . . . it's a total nightmare."

She glanced up, her eyes zeroing in on the beautiful cluster that should have been the prep school's fabulous five—Vanity, Dante, Christina, Pippa, and Max. Of course, now there were only four.

Bijou thought the survivors should be wearing dark glasses. Not because they'd been crying . . . but because the windows to their tortured souls looked too open to the horrors of the world. They were raw. They were exposed. They would never be the same again.

"We might think that we're not up for this," Bijou managed, her voice trembling. "Going on with our lives, rushing toward the exciting futures we've planned . . . in the aftermath of this heartbreak." Fighting back tears, she bit down on the inside of her cheek. "But we don't get a choice. There's only one way to face this. We have to go on . . ."

From: Max

You've either hooked up with a nympho or been de-
ported. Which is it? And if it's the nympho, I want her
number.

5:39 pm 7/24/05

chapter one

f or a model-thin girl, Vanity St. John could kick like a horse.

Dante Medina knew the look on his face was pure stupid as he went over the side of the boat, whipping through the wind with all the weight of a candy wrapper, still feeling the force of Vanity's rage attack in the concavity between his nipples. He hit the water with barely a splash.

"Crazy bitch!"

By the time Dante surfaced to scream out those words,

Vanity and the speeding Cobalt were at least a hundred yards gone.

His throat was instantly raw from the vocal cord strain, not to mention the violent intake of saltwater. Getting swallowed up by the wake upon entry had given him a cruel taste of the Atlantic.

He tried to assemble his thoughts, but the shock of the situation had barely registered. Struggling to tread water, he fought to keep his head above the surging tide. Jesus Christ, why had he refused to wear a life jacket? Oh, yeah. To be cool. Like that mattered now.

Dante's gaze remained locked onto the Cobalt as the boat continued to move farther and farther away. He kept expecting it to cut a wide turn and circle back. But now the watercraft was cruising beyond his sight line. A minute went by. And then another. Both made up the longest one hundred and twenty seconds of Dante Medina's life.

He experienced a steadily rising panic, his breath coming in gasping heaves as he eyeballed the distance to shore. The trip back to land was considerable. Vanity had hauled back the throttles and taken them at least two miles out, if not more. Everything in that direction was a blur. It looked like the skyscrapers of Miami Beach had fallen down.

Dante bobbed in the sea, waiting for the sick joke to

end. It had to be over any time now. His eyes would get a visual on the returning boat. Or maybe his ears would hear the rumble of the delicate fuel-injection engines. But the fearful moments just stretched on . . . and no sight or sound ever materialized. Shit! How could she just leave him out here in the middle of the freaking ocean?

He started to swim, cutting through the water with a determined stroke, wondering how life could possibly get any worse.

An emotionally bruising fight with his mother.

Passed out drunk on the beach and robbed of his wallet, cellphone, and dream watch.

Fired from his swim coaching job.

Thrown out on his ass by Simon St. John, the one man he'd been counting on to help him in the music business.

And then left for dead by Vanity, the first girl he'd felt a real connection to in a long time.

The sum of it all made Dante wish he could just sink to the bottom of the ocean. What was the point of living now?

But then the adrenaline of anger hit. He could actually feel it pumping through his veins as he huffed and puffed against the heavy current—swimming hard, but getting nowhere.

All of a sudden, the shoreline seemed more appealing

than the sea floor. Why? Because Dante was pissed off and wanted to show everyone that even though he may be down for the count, he was definitely not out of the fight.

Mentally, he checked off the haters.

First on his list was Rob Kelley, the do-nothing husband of Naomi Kelley, Hollywood's new Reese Witherspoon. Deep down, Dante had known that accepting the Chris "Iceman" Aire–designed watch would come back to haunt him. But he just couldn't resist the bling, especially after he tried on the piece, and it seemed to melt onto his wrist as if God intended it to be there.

That closet case was just pimping you out, dumb-ass, Dante cursed himself. How could he not have forecasted the outcome?

"This pool isn't getting a lot of use," Rob had said. "You should come by at night sometime. The volcano looks incredible then. You'd love it."

And then when Dante didn't show up, Rob had demonstrated his true inner bitch and called Sasha at Safe-Splash to accuse him of *stealing* the watch. Fast-forward just seconds after Sasha hung up with Rob. Dante's no-bullshit boss had no doubt called every one of his clients to explain why he wouldn't be coming back.

That's why Simon St. John had him pegged as a thug, a thief, and a bad influence on his daughter. If the man only knew. On any day of the week, Vanity had more vices than

Dante. Whatever. Simon St. John wasn't the last music executive on earth. Dante would make it without him.

And as for Vanity, Dante would make it without that psycho bitch, too. He doesn't call it love after one hookup, and she's ready to kill him? Jesus. Get some therapy, girl. It's not that deep.

Dante struggled to keep going, even as he felt like his body was dragging him down. Impulsively, he stopped to float on his back, working hard to peel off his jeans, then his shirt, which left him in nothing but white Calvin Klein boxer briefs. He could move now, though. His stroke was smoother, his kick faster. And he might be worn-out, exhausted, and sick from saltwater intake by the time he reached shore, but goddamn if he wasn't going to make it there.

Halfway in, the no-man's land of the vast ocean showed signs of intelligent life above water. A half-million-dollar custom Cigarette zoomed into view. It was the sweetest vision Dante had ever seen.

Upon sight of Dante, the young captain killed the 450 Mercruisers. "Yo! Dude! Need a little help?" the shirtless Hispanic man shouted, waving his hands, a diamond-encrusted, gold crucifix leaping on its chain and banging against his chest.

Two bikini-clad hotties flanked him on each side, both blonde, both surgically enhanced, or at the very least gloriously blessed. The girls didn't seem to know whether to laugh or to exhibit concern. So they covered both fronts, juxtaposing giggles with little gasps of somebody-help-him shock.

"What's up, man? You training for a triathlon or something?" the guy yelled, punctuating the question with a friendly laugh.

"Not intentionally," Dante hollered back. "Permission to come aboard!"

The young man tossed out a rescue tube attached to a rope.

Dante swam for the red lifeline, practically collapsing on top of it as the guy worked fast to pull him in.

"Were you actually swimming to shore?" the young man asked incredulously.

Dante shook his head up and down, his breathing still labored. "That was the plan."

His rescuer let down a small diving platform at the end of the boat, and the girls stepped forward to help him pull Dante out of the water.

When Dante connected with the solid surface, his body went limp. For a long moment, he just lay there on his back, relishing the fact that he didn't have to swim anymore.

"Nice trunks, dude," the guy cracked.

The girls giggled in response, even as they stole appreciative glances.

Dante looked down to see his sopping wet underwear,

which left nothing to the imagination. But he didn't even have the energy to modestly cover himself with his hands. So he just let the exhibitionism ride, grateful for the dry dock and concerned with nothing else at the moment.

"I'm Juan," the guy said.

"Dante." He flashed a quick peace sign. "I'll shake later, man. My arms feel like jelly."

"This is Leesa," Juan announced, gesturing to the girl on his left. "And that's Tahnee."

The girls grinned.

"Had I known the Coast Guard looked like this, I would've tried drowning a long time ago," Dante said.

"So what's your deal, man?" Juan asked.

Greedily, Dante took in more air. "I pissed off a girl and she kicked me out of her boat."

His explanation was met with dead silence.

"I'm serious," Dante insisted.

And then Juan, Leesa, and Tahnee erupted into a chorus of raucous laughter.

"You don't have the breakup conversation alone in shark-infested waters, man," Juan told him. "Talks like that are for outdoor cafés." He laughed again.

Dante rose up on his elbows and smiled at the scenery. The luxurious watercraft . . . the comely passengers . . . the scene was like a dream. "Guess I should pay attention. You sure know how to live."

"That I do, my friend," Juan said. "That I do." He appeared to be just a few years older than Dante, not a day past twenty-one.

Right away the questions were piling up for Dante. Who was this guy? And what did he do? Obviously, something that had him drowning in megabucks.

Juan lifted up the beige leather cushion on a sleek banquette, revealing storage underneath. He grabbed a pair of swim trunks and tossed the offering Dante's way.

Dante caught it midair. The suit was black and short on fabric, not quite a Speedo but not much more, with a white D&G BEACH logo racing down both sides. At first Dante hesitated. He preferred board shorts that stopped just above the knee. But right now anything was better than underwear. He sighed, murmured his thanks, and glanced around, wondering where to change.

Juan spun around to give Dante some privacy.

Leesa followed his lead.

But Tahnee kept a bold gaze glued onto Dante while he traded drenched underwear for skimpier swim trunks.

Initially, Dante experienced a pang of self-consciousness. The hip-hugging, ass-clinging, junk-enhancing suit was definitely a new look for him. But when he saw how much Tahnee seemed to approve, it took about a microsecond to get over the embarrassment.

Juan played with the stereo controls, and soon the irresistible groove of "La Tortura" by Shakira and Alejandro Sanz exploded from the bass-pounding sound system. "Pick a girl! Grab a beer! Let's party, man!" Juan shouted, instantly pairing off with Leesa.

Tahnee grinned, then went about the business of opening a Corona Light and stuffing a lime wedge inside the mouth of the bottle. She offered the drink to Dante.

He reached for it.

Teasingly, she pulled it away. "A kiss first."

Dante smiled, suddenly feeling his energy return. "You're a tough negotiator." He leaned in to claim her mouth, softly at first, then more aggressively. She tasted sweet, and the aroma of Coppertone emanated from her skin. Finally, he drew back. "Can I have my beer now?"

"Sure," Tahnee told him in a seductive whisper. "But just so you know, you'll have to earn every sip."

Dante took a generous swig, draining the Corona to the halfway mark. "There you go again with these impossible deal terms." And then his mouth found hers for round two, only more urgently this time.

Tahnee had an exquisite way of grinding against him, making Dante grow steadily harder where it mattered. Quite an achievement, considering the fact that he'd just swam until nearly passing out. Somewhere deep inside he felt a frisson of guilt. To be with Vanity . . . and now to be with Tahnee . . . did that make him a stud . . . or a jerk?

Suddenly, the anger at being kicked out of the boat and left in the ocean to become shark bait revved up his passion.

When Dante finally came up for air, his curiosity got the best of him. "So what's this Juan guy's story?"

"That's *Juan Barba,*" Tahnee said, as if the name alone explained everything.

Dante gazed at her blankly.

"He's, like, a Latin hip-hop/reggaetón star. You know that song, 'Sudores Nocturnos'?" She started to sing the hook and gyrate her hips back and forth.

Vaguely, Dante could place the melody. It'd been a minor hit in the States, which probably meant that in Latin America, the track was a monster.

"Are you a big Juan Barba fan?" Dante asked. "Is that why you're out here on his boat?"

Tahnee shrugged. "I'm sort of a video chick. Juan cast me as a dancer in his last clip. But mainly I just like to party . . . with him . . . and the occasional hot castaway." She glanced down, then up again, giving off a very sexy vibe.

"*Video chick,*" Dante repeated thoughtfully. "Is that a career path or something?"

Tahnee rolled her eyes, grinning. "If I get my shit together, it could be." She sighed. "Okay, there's, like, three levels. The lowest is the video ho. She's a total skank, basically a groupie, and she'll do anybody on the set to get a lead part or to just hang around a really big artist. Then there's the video chick, like me." She laughed a little. "I like to party, but only with the artist, you know? I mean, I'm not going to give it up for his bodyguard or some stupid assistant director. And then there's the video model. That's what I really want to be. I've just got to get my business plan together. She's, like, total class, and if you want her in your video, then you have to call her manager and agent and everything. They can make five thousand dollars a day."

"Major bling," Dante said.

"I know. It sure beats the three hundred bucks I got for my last gig."

He glanced around the posh surroundings. "At least you travel like a rich girl."

Tahnee gave him a curious look. "You must have really pissed off that girl to have her kick you out of a boat and haul ass to shore. The worst I've ever done to a guy is leave him in a restaurant. Of course, I did pour a drink over his head first."

Dante laughed. "Does that mean I'm still in dangerous waters? I thought I was safe."

Tahnee inched closer. "Do I look safe?"

Dante's eyes drifted to the breasts that were practically spilling out of her bathing suit top. "No, you look like trouble."

"The kind of trouble to avoid or the kind to get into?"

"Definitely the kind to get into." Dante leaned down to start up more kissing. With the beer gripped in one hand, he used his free fingers to undo the hook on Tahnee's bikini, keeping his tongue in her mouth the whole time. Nothing felt better than sexual multitasking.

But the balancing act proved too much, and they went tumbling down onto the leather banquette, a hot collision of wet lips, toned limbs, and sweat-slicked torsos. They landed in a heap and couldn't stop laughing.

The main casualty was the Corona Light, which survived the fall without breaking but spilled onto the immaculate deck.

Dante craned his neck to see Juan, who was lost in what looked to be the phenomenal oral attentions of Leesa.

The Latin star waved off any concern. "No worries, bro." And then he gave Dante the thumbs-up sign.

Tahnee glanced over at them and laughed. "Can you believe that? She's such a slut."

Dante hesitated a moment, searching deep into Tahnee's blue eyes, wondering if he was misreading the situation with her. Had he already gone too far?

Tahnee seemed to pick up on his inner doubt. She reached out to stroke his cheek. "Relax, Aquaman. I can be one, too."

Dante smiled the smile of a winner. "Promise?"

"Promise," Tahnee assured him.

And then Tahnee proceeded to make his bad day better.

There was one good thing about having a run of terrible luck.

It could definitely turn around.

From: Mimi

There's a VERY disturbing rumor going around.
Call me ASAP!!

6:22 pm 7/24/05

chapter two

Vanity watched them through the state-of-the-art viewfinder of the Nikon Venturer binoculars. Her heart pounded against her ribs as if fighting to escape.

"You son of bitch," Vanity hissed into the wind. Hormones that she never knew existed raged inside her.

For a fleeting moment, she communed with Lucifer, actually entertaining the thought of starting up the engines, pulling back the throttle, and using the Cobalt 343 as a deadly missile. She could ram the boat straight into the Cigarette and blow the disgusting scene to smithereens.

Slowly, Vanity lowered the binoculars, realizing that she'd been holding on to them with an intense, white-knuckled grip. Her hands were cramping. Her feelings were out of control.

First, there'd been that possessed Amazon moment when she kicked Dante out of the boat. But as soon as her fury subsided, Vanity had experienced a punishing regret that sent her racing back to retrieve him, all the while praying that he was safe. She'd actually thought that she loved him, too. So on some level, there should be relief in knowing that he was okay.

But the facts were too cruel for that. Here Vanity stood, the taste of Dante still in her mouth, while he carried on with another girl. She didn't feel love anymore. And she didn't feel grateful for seeing him alive, either. The only emotion she could conjure up was hatred.

Vanity raised the binoculars to take another look, then, thinking better of it, she put them down and picked up her Sidekick II to speed dial Dr. Parker. There were complicated issues to sort out. And if ever she needed an appointment with her therapist, then that time was right now. When it rang directly into voicemail, Vanity braced herself to sound better than she felt.

"Hi, Dr. Parker, it's me . . . Vanity. I know my regular appointment is a few days away, but some things have come up, and . . . I . . . really need to see you. Please call me if you can fit me in."

A text message from Mimi came through just as she was hanging up.

THERE'S A VERY DISTURBING RUMOR GOING AROUND. CALL ME ASAP!!

Vanity rolled her eyes. *Disturbing* to a personal publicist like Mimi Blair could mean being photographed wearing the same outfit twice. No matter, she was curious enough to want to know what people were saying about her, so she rang Mimi right away.

"We might have a *major* problem," Mimi said upon answering. This was a woman who didn't deal in hellos. She sledgehammered to the point of every conversation. "Did you make a sex tape with Jayson James?"

Vanity shut her eyes and slowly slid down into the cockpit. The sluice gates of fear opened up and began racing through her bloodstream.

"Are you there?" Mimi demanded.

"Yes," Vanity answered quietly. "I'm here."

"Did you make a sex tape with him?" Mimi asked again.

Vanity's memory vaulted back to that night at the Surfcomber. Oh God, she'd been in such a bad place emotionally *and* physically—lonely, depressed, wasted, stoned from the secondhand smoke of premium-blend pot.

"Well?"

"I don't know," Vanity said finally. "I suppose he could've had one of those cellphones that makes mini-movies. Or maybe he put a hidden camera somewhere. I was in no shape to notice."

"Guys are shit." Mimi sighed. "Let's not panic yet, though. I haven't talked to anyone who's actually seen this firsthand. There's just a story going around that he was showing it off at a party last night. But we need to get prepared just in case. Let me do some digging."

Vanity imagined the humiliating scenarios that were likely to unfold if a sex tape *did* exist. It would hit the Internet and spread like a plague. Video links. Screen captures. Blog mentions. Her lost night with Jayson "J.J." James would post *everywhere*. The name Vanity St. John would probably hit the top Google search hot list, too. And for all the wrong reasons.

"Mimi . . ." Vanity began, but her voice broke on the last syllable.

"If this is out there, then we'll come up with a plan of attack," Mimi said hotly, her voice ringing with steely reassurance.

Vanity thought of Paris Hilton and that infamous video *One Night in Paris* with Rick Salomon. Ultimately, the heiress had practically embraced the porn star exploits and increased her level of fame and notoriety exponentially. But that's *not* who Vanity wanted to be. After all, a scandal like this would basically follow her around for the rest of her life.

"I'll call you back with an update," Mimi said, signing off.

Vanity didn't scream out at the endless Atlantic. She didn't throw her mobile device into the water. She just started up the Cobalt and calmly piloted the watercraft back toward the Miami Beach Marina.

"My heart is blue . . . my heart is blue for you."

Completely lost in an iPod sonic assault, Shoshanna strutted toward the door, singing woefully off-key to what Max instantly recognized as "Rock & Roll Queen" by the Subways.

His precocious sister was dressed to incite a frat house riot in a two-sizes-too-small baby-doll tee emblazoned with the words PORN STAR across a braless, surgically enhanced chest. And this was over a skirt so short that it could easily be called a belt.

"Sho!" Max screamed, determined to break through the hard-charging guitars blasting her eardrums.

Shoshanna halted in a huff, reluctantly hitting pause on the music device as she gave her older-by-two-years brother an impatient, expectant look.

"Aren't you forgetting something?" Max asked.

"Like what?"

"Your lamp post," he answered. "You'll need something to lean against while you stand on the corner and wait for your pimp to drive up and say, 'Bitch, get in my car.'"

Shoshanna shook her head, unfazed. "Oh, is that supposed to be funny?"

Max chuckled to himself. "Actually, it was pretty good. You have to admit that." Then his smile fell into a firm line. "Seriously, though, put on some actual clothes. You're not going out like that."

"Our stepmonster said that I looked cute!"

"People say all sorts of things after four martinis," Max countered. "As a general rule, don't believe any of them."

Shoshanna splayed out her hands in a faux model stance. "I don't get it. What's wrong with this?"

"Toosmalltootighttooshortnobra," Max said in a lightning fast clip. "And don't get me started on your cute slogan." He shook his head. "'Porn star'? Come on, Sho. Save a little shock value for when you turn sixteen."

"It's a joke."

"Yeah, well, on a fat girl with acne, it'd be funny. On you, the typical guy might consider it worth the jail time." Max moved in front of the door and folded his arms. "Go change. *Now.*"

Defiantly, Shoshanna whipped her hair around. "You can't make me."

Max gave her a menacing look. "You're right. But I *can* ban you from my parties and my poker games."

"God! I feel like I'm on *Seventh Heaven* or something!"

She started to stomp up the stairs, then halted with exasperation. "What am I supposed to wear?"

"I don't know. Right now you look like a teenage hooker, so even if you come back down dressed like a slut, I'd still consider that a major improvement."

"You're *such* a dick."

"I know. It's in the official job description for big brothers. I have to fulfill my duty."

"Maybe I should give this 'porn star' shirt to Vanity," Shoshanna said, sneering devilishly. "I hear it's no joke to her."

All of a sudden, Max felt his body go cold. "What's that supposed to mean?"

"My friend Yummy was at a party last night, and she said J.J. was there showing everybody a tape of him having sex with Vanity."

"Son of a bitch!" Max nearly spat. One thing was certain: If Yummy Larocca knew about it, then the rest of the world would soon follow. No detail was too small or too private for that little bitch's blog.

Shoshanna peeled off the thin cotton shirt and covered her breasts with one arm. "Here! Give it to her yourself!" And with that, she flung the top at Max's face and raced up the stairs, giggling.

Max caught the garment and just stood there, preoccupied, tormented, and conflicted. He was all about business. That's why a select few called him Baby Donald, after Donald Trump. Let other guys his age have their sports heroes and fawn over rap stars. Max preferred the billionaire blowhard.

J.J.'s video had the potential to be a sweet cash windfall, the kind that the Donald would truly appreciate. It'd make the money from Max's poker games and theme parties look like revenue from a kid's lemonade stand. What was it about seeing famous people having sex? Everybody wanted a look. It was the ultimate voyeurism. And the ultimate humiliation, too. How would Vanity deal with that?

Oh, shit. Max was already starting to crack under the pressure of guilt. So much for a kill-or-be-killed business edge. Maybe he didn't have the heart of a corporate assassin after all. Christ. At the end of the day, did that make him a sappy little twat or a decent guy who could listen to his conscience? Maybe a bit of both.

Shoshanna came bounding down the stairs and stopped on the last step. "Happy now?"

Max gave her a quick once-over.

At best, his sister had managed a minor improvement. Now her shirt carried the phrase YOU DON'T HAVE TO GET ME DRUNK, and her low-rise jeans revealed a peek of thong underwear.

"Compared to your last outfit, it's almost a wholesome

look," Max said. "If I didn't know any better, I'd swear you were going to a Bible study."

Shoshanna rolled her eyes, grinning. "I don't think Yummy has that book." She started for the door.

"Where are you going?"

"Clubbing with the fake IDs you made for us."

"Remind me to smash my head with a hammer for doing that."

"Wasn't it you who told me that I was safer in a bar with a thirty-year-old man than alone in a basement with any guy your age?"

"That does sound like something I'd say," Max admitted.

"Okay, then. You can relax now, right?" She laughed and slipped out.

He sighed and tracked down his keys, ready for some fun of his own. If he couldn't screw Vanity, then he might as well screw some other girl. Besides, a hot one was on her way to a hotel right now, operating under the false assumption that Max could help her get cast in a movie.

He laughed a little, relieved that his inner sleazy bastard was still alive and kicking.

The vague sense of imminent doom was paralyzing, and for the longest time, Vanity just sat in the packed marina parking lot, safely ensconced in her Mercedes SL500.

She dreaded the call from Mimi.

She dreaded the next encounter with her father.

She dreaded ever seeing Dante Medina again.

On a sudden impulse, she called Max. A conversation with her oldest friend was probably the only thing in the world Vanity wasn't dreading right now. He picked up, and she could barely hear his greeting above the blaring NWA track, "A Bitch Iz a Bitch."

"Max!" Vanity cried in frustration. "Turn that shit down!"

"Sorry," he chirped just as the sonic boom ended. "I'm pumping old-school rap today. *Straight outta Compton!*"

Vanity rolled her eyes. As if this rich white boy knew *anything* about life in South Central Los Angeles. "I need a laugh, Max," she groaned. "Tell me something funny."

"Okay, two child molesters walk into a bar," Max said, not missing a beat.

"Please."

"This joke is funny as shit," Max insisted. "Unless you're an incest survivor. Then it might hit too close to home. But it's still funny. Okay, so the first child molester asks the bartender for a Shirley Temple—"

"Stop!" Vanity cut in, even though she was laughing as she protested. "I don't want to hear this! God! You're sick!"

Max cackled. "You're the one laughing at the joke before the punch line. I think *you're* the sick one."

"For calling you in the first place, maybe I am."

"Have you heard from Dante?" Max asked. "He hasn't answered my texts."

"That's because the idiot passed out on the beach and got himself mugged," Vanity announced bitterly. "They took his phone, wallet, and that stupid diamond watch."

"Shit!" Max exclaimed. "Are you serious?"

"Don't worry. He wasn't hurt. He slept through the whole thing like a skid-row bum."

"You sound pissed off," Max observed. "Let me guess—he came first and then lost interest. You have to remember that he's the son of a maid. There are some manners he's probably unaware of. It's not just table etiquette that the poor have trouble with."

Vanity shook her head in disbelief. "Sometimes talking to you is pure torture."

"Why? Because I'm not afraid to speak the truth?"

"That's hardly the truth," Vanity argued with good humor. "It's just offensive."

"Usually, the truth is," Max said.

Vanity eased her seat back into the reclining position and closed her eyes. "So what are we doing tonight? I don't feel like going home."

"I've got plans."

Struck by the odd tone in Max's voice, Vanity opened her eyes. There was a time when he would've dropped anything to be with her. "What kind of plans?"

"Just stuff," he answered evasively. "Why don't you call Christina? I'm sure she's home alone waiting for the phone to ring like a fat girl on New Year's Eve."

"Oh, that's nice," Vanity murmured. "Did you pick that up in your sensitivity training class?"

Max laughed. "A hundred bucks says she answers after the first ring."

"Whatever." Vanity sighed. "So what kind of 'stuff' has you tied up tonight?"

"The kind we don't do anymore."

"Poor girl," Vanity murmured. "She has no idea how disappointed she's going to be."

Max laughed. "Good one. Actually, she called *me* for another dose, and I'm only giving it to her because the girl's wild in bed. She doesn't just lay there like a Terri Schiavo." He pretended to clear his throat. "Sort of like one of my old girlfriends."

"Oh, you prick!" Vanity shot back, amused and insulted at the same time.

Max laughed again. "What? I didn't mention any names."

Vanity eased her seat up to the driving position and turned the key over. The German engine purred to life.

Boys. They were so stupid most of the time, only giving real thought to situations that might benefit their dicks.

Her destination unknown, Vanity coasted out of the marina lot and pointed the car in the direction of South Beach. "Can I ask you something?"

"Fire away."

"Would you ever tape yourself with a girl without her knowledge?"

Max fell eerily silent.

"I take it that means yes." Vanity huffed. "Is every guy in the world an absolute pig?"

"Either that, or he's obsessed with *Star Wars.* I think you'd prefer the pigs."

"So you've actually done that to a girl," Vanity snapped, her tone full of accusation.

"Yes, but once I saw my come face on video, I destroyed the evidence and never played amateur porn star again."

No matter how hard she tried to resist, Vanity started to laugh. "I'm being serious, Max."

"So am I. You've seen the look on my face when I come. It's hideous. Whenever I nail a girl, I should probably be wearing a *Phantom of the Opera* mask."

Vanity was smiling, her mood levitated by talking to Max as she knew it would be, but the gnawing belief that there was, in fact, a tape out there of her and J.J. had reached a sudden fever pitch. Her heart was racing, her body was shaking, and her foot was heavy on the accelerator, as if road speed might help her escape the inevitable.

Finally, she gave voice to the fear. "There's a rumor going around that J.J. made a tape of us."

Max fell silent.

"Have you heard about it?" Vanity asked.

His silenced continued.

"It's true, isn't it?" She held her breath for the denial, and when that didn't come the tears did. "Oh God, I knew it. When Mimi called, I *knew* it was true. I could feel it in my gut." She pushed a tendril of hair away from her eyes. "I can't handle this right now. I just can't."

"Don't freak," Max said, trying his best to be comforting. "People will look at it once on their computers. Guys will wish they could be J.J., and girls will be jealous about how hot you are. And then it'll be forgotten."

The intensity of Vanity's crying jag increased. "I feel like everything is falling apart, you know? Taking a simple breath is *painful*. Sometimes I just want it to stop. It's like . . . I don't want to be around for this anymore."

"You're talking crazy," Max said. His tone was gravely serious, a rarity for him. "Where are you right now? I'll come get you. We'll go somewhere and talk."

"Forget it. You've got a girl to screw, remember?" She hung up and twisted the stereo dial to a deafening volume. Madonna's "What It Feels Like for a Girl" exploded from the XM station.

She drove faster . . . and faster . . . and faster, weaving in and out of traffic, attacking the road like an after-midnight drag racer. It was so strange. The car was almost out of control—just like her life—but Vanity felt totally in charge. Perhaps for the very fist time.

Suddenly, she saw it . . . up ahead, the eighteen-wheeler with the fuel cargo. It was in her path for a reason tonight. All she had to do was punch the accelerator, run the red light, and leave the rest up to God.

And then Vanity St. John closed her eyes. As her foot pressed down, she experienced a nanosecond of deceptive calm. There was no turning back. It would all be over soon.

From: J.J.

We better move fast, man. My cell's blowing up about
this sex vid!

6:47 pm 7/24/05

chapter three

max knocked back a shot of vanilla-flavored Grey Goose, then tried to reach Vanity again. Still no answer. *Shit.* Girls could be so freaking dramatic.

"Pick up the phone, bitch!" he yelled. But just like the last dozen attempts, the connection went straight to voicemail.

Frustrated, Max tossed his Sidekick onto the bed. It bounced off the mattress and went flying, hitting the grasslike cloth on the wall before landing under a sleek, black-lacquered bench.

The goal tonight had been to kick it at the Raleigh Hotel in South Beach. He had the Ocean Front King all to himself. The plan was to get laid, party up, and sleep until noon. But Max could barely stand still, and, amazingly, sex happened to be the last thing on his mind.

He paced the brown-and-ocher terrazzo floors, jittery as hell, like a nervous cat in a cage. It didn't help that his mind was playing out a thousand nightmare images. Something about Vanity's choice of words and the sound of her voice chilled him to the very marrow of his bones.

Three knocks rapped the door.

Max took the time to pour another vodka shot before answering. After all, he knew who it was. Standing on the other side would be Jaclyn Angel, actress/model/whore. So why rush?

Finally, he flung open the door.

"I could get used to this," Jaclyn cooed in a melodic singsong, strutting inside the room wearing a standard-issue Sluts "R" Us package—fake tits, low-cut top, a skirt that barely skimmed the lower reaches of her butt cheeks, and towering heels.

In one hand she clutched a rhinestone-encrusted Hello Kitty bag, and in the other she carried the rumpled script pages of the bogus Max Biaggi vehicle that would never get past this all-important development stage: Casting Couch Heaven for Star's Horny Son.

"I've been practicing my lines," Jaclyn announced. She robbed Max of his shot and downed the Grey Goose like it was a splash of Gatorade. Sweeping a tongue over her plump lips, she smiled and passed back the empty glass. "But I didn't have the complete script, so I don't really understand my character. To give my best performance, I need to know who she is."

"This isn't a Sundance film, sweetheart. In the opening scene, the leading man picks you up at an airport bar. After that, you're killed in the first action set piece."

"Oh," Jaclyn murmured, deflated but still interested in the role. She moved toward Max. "I was just searching for my motivation. But I guess I'm not going to find it on the page." Hooking her fingers underneath the waistband of his Rock & Republic jeans, she gave him a big, toothy grin.

It always amazed Max that girls who wanted to be actresses chose breast implants over dental work. Jaclyn Angel might have a body for sin, but the hopeful starlet with the bad stage name had a smile for radio. In a world of HDTV, she'd be lucky to get a callback for a crowd scene.

Even with her talented hands snaking down to bring him to life, Max didn't feel so much as a twitch in response. To describe him as flaccid was being charitable. Still, the failure to launch didn't bother him, because by this point during their last meeting, he already had Jaclyn bent over the sofa and was ramming her with all the motivation she'd ever need. But circumstances were different tonight.

Max gently pushed her hands away. "Sorry. I can't do this tonight. Something's come up."

At first, she looked crestfallen.

Max retrieved her purse and script pages, then attempted to usher her out the door.

Jaclyn resisted, turning angry on a dime. "What kind of bullshit audition is this?"

Max groaned. "Now's not the time to play your big scene, baby. We'll do this again later."

But Jaclyn stood firm. "I want to talk to someone else involved with the movie."

Max put a hand on the small of her back and pressed forward. "Okay, I'll have the executive producer give you a call. How does that sound?"

"Like a load of crap!" One beat. "You're not even a real casting director, are you?"

"What can I say? It's a tough business. Filled with sharks."

"Not to mention losers on the make!" With that, Jaclyn ripped up her script and littered the pieces across the floor. "Screw you!"

"You did that last time," Max shot back. "And very well, too. I have to give higher marks for the sex than for the acting, though. Your line readings were a little wooden."

Thwack! The slap across the face came hard, fast, and without warning.

Max brought a hand to his cheek, which began to throb instantly. "But the acting's getting better," he cracked. "I actually believe that you don't like me right now. Good job, baby."

Jaclyn stormed out, slamming the door behind her.

Max knew he'd just given enhanced meaning to the term "major-league asshole," but he didn't care. Miami was chockablock with Jaclyn Angel types. And right now his brain was wrapped around a special girl, a one of a kind, a true original . . . Vanity St. John.

He retrieved his Sidekick from the floor and tried her number again without success. "Come on, girl! Answer your goddamn phone!"

Beads of sweat formed on Max's forehead as terrible fears began to register in earnest. The truth was, unlike most people, Vanity had the balls to take herself out. People said suicide was a coward's escape, and at the end of the day, that was true. But the initial act itself, that final move, the decision on how to go, the capacity to actually carry it out . . . well, that required some guts. And Vanity had them.

He thought about his gorgeous friend. Usually, Max kept feelings at bay. Sentimentality was for losers. Ditto guilt. They were signs of weakness that did you no good. But right now he couldn't help giving in to both.

Max and Vanity shared the same wrecked childhood. Selfish mothers who abandoned them. Ambivalent fathers who showed their love with car keys and credit cards. Privately, they both hurt from this. Publicly, they both cut through life with a ruthless self-confidence that belied their secret insecurities.

Max couldn't imagine his life without Vanity in it. Over the years, while other friendships had faded in, burned out, or savagely imploded, Vanity had always been there. Like his sister, Shoshanna, she was a consistent presence that kept him going, a source of light that made him feel secure.

He sank down onto the bed and buried his face in his hands, the meeting in the park with J.J. playing back in his mind like a horror movie. To think that for one second he'd seriously considered selling out his friend consumed Max with a venomous self-loathing.

At first, he tried to convince himself that it was all bullshit, that when it came down to the wire, he wouldn't have been able to go through with the betrayal. But deep down, Max knew otherwise. His dark side could creep up at unexpected times, often with a force all its own.

Max had never done the prayer thing. That was for the religious. He was a believer, but conversations with God seemed meaningless. In a world of natural disasters and kids strapping bombs to their chests in the Middle East, how could he shout out for his mother to call him on his birthday?

But right now Max was praying. More than that, he

was negotiating. If he found Vanity safe and sound, then he'd kiss the sex tape millions good-bye. In fact, he'd set up J.J. to fail so spectacularly that instead of rolling in megabucks, the third-tier male model would be swimming in debt. And Max would call an end to these casting couch schemes, too. There were plenty of *legitimate* industry types out there taking advantage of desperate actresses, so Max's bogus movie trickeroo was just adding insult to injury.

He glanced upward, as if in conference with the Almighty. It wasn't exactly a vow of hunger. But these were ultimate sacrifices in the decadent world of Max Biaggi Jr. And God had to know that. Everything was relative, right?

Suddenly, John Carpenter's *Halloween* theme cut into the silence. The Sidekick ringtone gave Max a jolt, but he recovered quickly, filled with the vibrant hope that Vanity might be calling back. One look and he saw that it was Pippa. His spirits crashed. "What's up?"

"Don't you love me anymore?" Pippa whined. "You haven't called me all bloody day." She could sense Max smiling over the phone. Her hot British accent did it to them every time.

"Have you heard from Vanity?" he asked.

"Not today."

Max sighed.

Pippa picked up on his inner torment. "What's wrong?"

"Maybe nothing . . . but . . . I'm not going to be able to relax until I know she's okay." He relayed the story about Vanity's disturbing phone rant and her distress over the J.J. sex-tape rumor.

"What a wanker!" Pippa cried. "Somebody should cut off his 'nads and feed them to a goat!"

Max laughed a little. "I hadn't thought of that as a course of action, but you've got my vote."

A few beats of silence passed.

Finally, Pippa broke it. "Do you truly believe that she could . . ."

"Who really knows for sure?" Max answered. "I just know that I've never heard her talk like that before, and it sounded . . . ominous."

"Have you ever . . . ?" Pippa started, then broke off.

"Have I ever what?" Max pressed.

She hesitated. "Thought about it."

"No," he said matter-of-factly. "Mainly because of my sister, I guess. I could never do something like that to her, so why even think about it? Honestly, though, I've never felt that depressed. I mean, some screwed-up shit has happened to me, but nothing that ever made me think about killing myself."

Pippa was quiet.

"Have you?" Max asked.

"A few times . . . back in England," she admitted. "For

a long period it seemed like nothing would ever get better, and then, all of a sudden, it did. That's the thing, you know? Things get better. They always do. You just have to ride out the storm." She paused a beat. "I still can't believe you've never thought about it."

"I haven't," Max said. "Not even once."

"Is it a girl thing or something?" Pippa wondered with half a laugh.

"I wouldn't say that. Every year, four times as many guys die from suicide."

"That's a crazy statistic."

"Most girls attempt to kill themselves, but guys get the job done the first time."

"Of course." Pippa sniffed. "Boys are so performance oriented." Then she sighed. "It's just hard to believe that Vanity of all people could feel so desperate. She seems to have such a perfect life."

"The grass is always greener . . ." Max murmured, trailing off before finishing the cliché.

"I suppose she *is* the proverbial poor little rich girl," Pippa said, her words spilling out in a nastier tone than she intended.

"What?" Max's voice was punchy. "People with money can't have problems?"

His defensive question stung. Pippa had grown up with the best of everything. Being part of the struggling class was still new to her. In fact, she still thought of herself as an upper-class girl, only one experiencing a period of awkward transition. But Max seemed to be making a point that he and Vanity were in a totally different league.

"You sound like a Democrat," he went on.

Pippa wanted to bang down the receiver. "I'm not some ghetto girl! I know what it's like to have money, Max. I've spent most of my time on this bloody earth swimming in it. And all I know is this—anything that life throws at you is easier to handle if you've got a secure future and loads of cash in the bank."

"Spoken like a true bling bitch who thinks a new Prada bag is a Band-Aid for everything."

Now Pippa was seething. Max had no idea. The mouthy little bastard didn't have a clue. To see the words "insufficient funds" on your ATM receipt. To wonder if college was even a possibility. To want something in a store so badly that the urge to steal it became as pronounced as a muscle ache.

Money can't buy happiness.

Pippa hated that old sentiment. What bullshit it was. The rich held on to the belief because they wanted dibs on misery, too. And as for the poor people who bought into that crappy line. . . well, they needed something to provide comfort to their miserable lives. Religion couldn't do all the heavy lifting.

The truth was, a fistful of dollars *could* buy happiness. Money was the open sesame to freedom and choices, because without it, you had neither. Without money, you went from a mansion in England to a shoddy cottage off Miami Beach. Without money, you bummed rides or shamefully took the bus while the movie star's son and the music mogul's daughter zipped around in their Porsche and Mercedes. Without money, you promised to pay your friends back for a movie ticket, a Starbucks, or a sushi dinner—and then you prayed that they wouldn't remember the debt. Without money, you just might walk into a strip club called Cheetah and agree to dance naked for an audience of creepy guys.

Max could call her a bling bitch. Pippa didn't care. Because she knew what she really was—a survivor, and a couple of shifts at the Gap followed by a lousy paycheck a few weeks later would hardly keep her alive. Stripping was the quickest way to make the money she needed. Now *that* was a reason to kill yourself. But Max would never understand her situation. The bratty bloke probably didn't even know what a bank was. Cash and credit were just always there for him, like candy in a bowl.

"I just hope she doesn't do anything stupid, you know?" Max said, ending the tense silence.

Pippa could hear real fear in his voice. Suddenly, her own issues were dwarfed by the sudden realization that

Vanity really might become one of those ghastly statistics. "Well, we can't just sit here and imagine a million scenarios!" she erupted. "We should go out there and look for her, call everyone she knows, do *something!*"

Max rose up with a start. That was precisely the kick in the ass he needed. "I'm coming to pick you up," he said, signing off just as another call flashed from a number he didn't recognize. Bracing himself for bad news, he switched over. "This is Max."

"You won't believe what happened to me today." It was Dante, giving off top-of-the-world vibrations.

"You don't sound like a dude who just got bling-jacked on the beach," Max said.

"So you heard?" Dante shouted over throbbing Latin music in the background.

"Yeah, I got the Cliffs Notes version."

"Man, that seems like a lifetime ago," Dante said, practically dismissing the incident altogether. "I got rescued by some new friends. We're jamming at Iguana. Come out and party with us. A new girl just joined our group. Her name's January."

"Are you hot?" a female voice screamed into the phone.

Dante laughed. "That's her. Come on, man. She needs someone to keep her company."

On any other night, Max would be down for industrial-strength fun. But not on this one. "Have you heard from Vanity?"

"Screw that bitch," Dante said hotly. "She kicked me out of her boat and left me in the middle of the ocean. If Juan Bar—"

"I'm worried about her, man," Max cut in. *Seriously.* When I talked to her last, she sounded strange. It was crisis-line shit. And now I can't reach her." He glanced around at the pristine Art Deco elegance of the hotel room, then fell back onto the bed and closed his eyes. Pippa was right. Things *would* get better. He just hoped that Vanity realized that.

"I'm sure she's fine," Dante said dismissively. "Chicks love drama. You know that."

Max rose up and made a fast track toward the elevator. "Well, I can't just brush this off, man. I'm heading over to fetch Pippa. We're going to stop by her house, hop around some clubs, see if we can run up on anyone who might know where she is."

"That's exactly what she wants you to do," Dante argued. "Remember this conversation when you find her dancing in a VIP section with a Lebanese club promoter."

"Thanks for the support, asshole!" Max shouted. "You know what? I'd kick your sorry ass out of a boat, too!"

"Dude, take it easy. All I'm saying is—"

"You weren't on the phone with the girl. I was. I listened

to the shit she was saying. I heard the desperation in her voice. It freaked me out, man. I'm not playing around here!"

"This sounds deep," Dante said quietly.

"It is," Max confirmed. "So maybe you could put your dick back in your pants and take me seriously for a second."

"Okay, man. You've got my attention. What can I do?"

"Shit, I don't know," Max answered, rushing toward the valet station to push a ticket into the hand of a bored-looking attendant. "Put a move on it. I'm in a hurry."

"Maybe I should get with Christina," Dante suggested. "That way we could cover more ground."

"Yeah, okay," Max muttered. "Stay in touch." He hung up and stood there, anxiety on a slow boil as he wondered why the parking doofus was taking so goddamn long.

Finally, the Porsche rolled up to a sharp stop.

Max flicked the idiot a ten-dollar bill and strapped himself in, burning rubber out of the Raleigh, almost clipping a BMW roadster as he roared onto Collins Avenue, rocking "Best of You" by the Foo Fighters and singing along with the band's gravel-voiced lead singer, Dave Grohl.

"It's real, the pain you feel/The life, the love/You die to heal . . ."

Christina was slavishly sketching an image of Vanity from an *Elle* pictorial when her cellular rang. The number on display mystified her. "Hello?"

"Hey, it's Dante."

She was stunned to hear from him but instantly thrilled, too, as it made her feel connected to the group. "Hi," she answered, working hard to keep her response tempered. Dante, Max, Vanity, and Pippa were so cool in the ways of social interaction, and she was so . . . not cool about it. "What's up?"

"Nothing, I hope. I just talked to Max. He's worried about Vanity. Thinks she might be having some sort of breakdown."

Christina's grip tightened on the mobile. Instantly, her mind referenced their encounter at the Shore Club just a month ago, the first time that she and Vanity had really talked, a moment that she replayed over and over again. That wonderful day had solidified her feelings for the beautiful and famous girl, upgrading them from secret crush to secret love.

Just so you know, I'm totally screwed-up.

Vanity had said it. And Christina had assumed that it was just self-deprecating girl-to-girl banter. *You think you're a mess? No, honey, I'm a mess.* But right now she was feeling a rush of irrational guilt. Maybe that admission had been a subtle cry for help. And Christina missed it. Even worse, what if Vanity thought that she ignored it? Oh God, Vanity had to know that Christina cared!

"She's not picking up her cell," Dante was saying.

"Max and Pippa are heading out to look for her in the obvious places. I thought we could—"

"I'll do anything," Christina cut in. "I have to—I mean, *we* have to find her."

"This sounds insane, but I'm coming off a rough night, and I don't even know where my damn car is. Can you come get me? I'm at Iguana. It's off Mill—"

"I know where it is. I'll leave right now." She hung up, snatched her purse, and frantically searched around for her keys. Why didn't she just leave them in the same place? Suddenly, she heard a glorious jingle-jangle as she kicked at a small pile of clothes on the floor of her bedroom.

The phone rang again. Christina's heart lurched. And then she saw who it was. Her stupid mother! She took a deep breath, fighting for calm. "Hi, Mom."

"I've got wonderful news," Paulina Perez said. "I just received an official endorsement from the Miami Baptist Association, and we're all going out to celebrate. How does Italian sound? I know how much you love Café Prima."

Christina managed a realistic groan. "I've felt awful all day. I can't even imagine food, especially Italian. Have fun, though. I'm just going to try to get some sleep."

"Oh, no, what's wrong?" Paulina asked.

Christina rolled her eyes at the concerned mother bit. These days Paulina only cared about one thing—her bid to enter the Senate race. "It's nothing serious. Just a stomach bug, I guess."

"Well, get some rest, okay?"

"I will. Congratulations."

"Thanks, sweetie. Feel better."

Christina signed off and raced into the garage. Lying to her mother was the only way to go. Paulina would never allow her to drive around after dark with a boy like Dante to hunt down a possibly suicidal celebutante. But that's precisely what she intended to do.

Traffic was bumper-to-bumper. Max cut down 17th Street/Hank Meyer Boulevard until he hit Alton Road. But what had been cars moving in a slow crawl became total gridlock. Drivers played out their frustrations with a cacophony of horn blasts. Max joined in, punching the steering wheel to make noise as he leaned out the window, craning his neck to get a beat on the source of the holdup.

Police, ambulance, and fire truck sirens screamed in the night. Flashing red-and-blue lights lit up the Miami sky.

Max waited, his fingers tapping a nervous rhythm on the dash. Five minutes became ten. The wheels of the Porsche hadn't rolled forward so much as an inch. He snatched his Sidekick and rang Pippa.

She picked up with a breathless, "Have you heard anything?"

"No," Max said irritably. "And now I'm in the middle of a total traffic fu—"

A motorcycle cop zoomed past, racing between lanes, missing bike-to-car contact by mere millimeters.

"Shit!" Max exclaimed. "Some Erik Estrada almost clipped my driver's side mirror!"

"Who?" Pippa asked.

"Didn't they show *CHiPS* in England?"

"Never heard of it."

"One night we'll get drunk and watch a marathon," Max promised. "You don't know what you're missing." He hopped out of the car and started down the path led by the Ponch wannabe.

"Hey, buddy!" the motorist behind him called out angrily. "If you're not here to drive when this line starts moving, my front bumper will do it for you!"

Max responded with an imperious wave of his hand. "Asshole!"

In answer, Max shot up two middle fingers, never even bothering to turn around.

Another road jam victim was just returning to his vehicle, a gleaming new Jaguar XJ in metallic red.

"What's going on up there?" Max asked.

The silver-haired corporate type, a near dead ringer for CNN's Anderson Cooper, shook his head with equal parts sadness and annoyance. "Looks like a young girl went head-on with a semi. It's a fuel truck, too, so we may be here for a while."

Max froze. His stomach did a complete revolution. A stark fear seized him, bringing with it the sensation that his heart had stopped. All of a sudden, he just knew. The girl in question was Vanity. He took off, sprinting toward the scene, mind and body in tumult.

When he saw the demolished Capri blue Benz, he halted. It took a long moment for the full impact of the devastating reality to sink in.

And then, right there in the middle of the street, Max dropped down to his knees.

From: J.J.

Have u heard the shit about Vanity's accident? It's all
over the news. We can make a killing if we act now!

2:07 am 7/25/05

chapter four

max, Pippa, Dante, and Christina were sitting shell-shocked at Gino's, a New York-style pizza joint on Washington Avenue. Even now, in the wee hours of the morning, the place hummed with a steady stream of shift workers and club warriors.

"I just don't understand why," Pippa remarked, filling the somber airspace.

Max shot Dante a meaningful look as he downed a buttery garlic knot.

"What?" Pippa wondered, fixing her stare on Max, then switching it to Dante.

But Dante just played with the fuzz on his chin and avoided eye contact, looking guilty and miserable.

Max knew that it wasn't fair to put him on the spot,

but he proceeded to anyway. "What happened on the boat?"

"You're blaming me for this, too?" Dante responded hotly.

Max held up both hands in a gesture of mock protection. "Easy, turbo—I'm just asking a question."

Dante rubbed tired, bloodshot eyes. "There was an intense scene at Vanity's house with her dad."

Christina spoke up. "More intense than his scene at the hospital?"

They had all been there at Mount Sinai Medical Center when Simon St. John nearly attacked Dante, calling him a "punk thief" and threatening him with bodily harm if he didn't leave immediately.

Max had stepped in to stop the altercation before it came to blows. But Vanity's father had been relentless and refused to calm down until Dante left altogether. It'd been such an embarrassing display. And you didn't have to be Dr. Phil to pinpoint what was happening psychologically. Simon St. John was just channeling all the inner guilt he felt for not being there as a parent into outer rage toward Dante, whom his daughter had only known for just over a month.

Sure, go ahead, asshole, Max thought bitterly. Blame anyone but yourself. It was the same kind of pathetic bullshit that his own father would probably try to pull. Suddenly, Max was struck by a morbid realization, which left him wondering.

Did Dante and Christina have it easier? After all, they'd both lost their fathers at a young age. At least that set them free to construct a fantasy image of how their dads might have been. Was mourning a dead father less painful than dealing with the constant letdowns of one still living?

Max nodded at Dante. "So what happened?"

"He found us in her bedroom," Dante began softly. "It wasn't what it looked like. But the guy went crazy. Vanity tried to reason with him, and they got in a huge fight. He ended up calling her a slut. After that, we left."

Pippa rolled her eyes. "Just the sort of words you want to hear from *Daddy.*"

"Yeah," Max put in. "That wouldn't screw up a teenage girl at all." One beat. "Parents can be so goddamn lame."

There was a collective moment of silence that seemed to imply unanimous agreement.

"She took me straight to the marina," Dante went on. "And before I knew it, we were way out in the water and all over each other. I don't think we even realized what was happening . . . it was just, you know, two desperate people." He played with the ice in his Coke. "I can't even remember what I said exactly . . . after we were done . . . but . . . it wasn't the right thing, obviously. She kicked me out of the boat. *Literally.* I mean, I took a hit right here to the chest." He placed a hand on his pectorals for emphasis. "And then she took off and never came back."

"Well, how did you make it back to shore?" Pippa's tone was incredulous.

"Another boat came along," Dante said.

Pippa glanced over to Max. "Well, if there's anyone to blame here, I say it's J.J. and that stupid video."

Dante narrowed his eyes. "What video?"

Max stifled a groan and shook his head regretfully. "There's a sex tape out there," he explained. "She was wasted and had no idea that they were being taped. J.J.'s looking to make some money off of it, and word got out. She was pretty upset about it."

"Yeah, enough to go kill herself," Christina blurted. Suddenly, her eyes welled up with tears and she bolted from the table.

Pippa shot up, trailing Christina as the distraught girl fled the restaurant.

Miserably, Max shoved some pizza into his mouth.

"J.J.'s a friend of yours, isn't he?" Dante asked pointedly.

"He's played poker at my house. We've gotten shit-faced a few times. But I wouldn't call him a friend."

"Have you seen it?"

Max gave him a severe nod. "Not all of it, but enough to know that it won't go away anytime soon."

"I should track him down and beat that motherfu—"

"Let me handle this," Max cut in. "Barrio justice won't work with this dude. Besides, J.J.'s stoned all the time. He probably wouldn't feel a thing. Anyway, I don't think you could take him."

Dante glanced up, amusingly unamused.

Max smirked a little. But deep inside, his guts were twisting. He had to find a way to stop J.J. This sex tape shit had to be buried. Max owed Vanity that much. Otherwise, he would never forgive himself.

"Man, this is so fucked-up," Dante murmured.

"Truer words have never been spoken," Max said.

"Christina, wait!" Pippa cried.

She was running. She didn't know where. She didn't know why. There was a pull on her vintage practically moth-eaten sweater and finally Christina stopped.

Tears were rolling down her cheeks. The Miami night would fast become a Miami morning. She missed Vanity already. There was a void. Christina could *feel* it. The image of the crushed Mercedes wouldn't leave her. She tried to shut off her mind to the horrifying visual, but it haunted her like a demon.

"It's okay," Pippa assured her. "It's been a long night. Just try to take some deep breaths."

Christina shook her head, as if still not believing the nightmare. "They said she just drove straight into the truck. I heard a witness talking about it on the news at the hospital. She didn't even try to stop . . ."

Her voice trailed off as she tried to imagine Vanity's last thoughts before the accident. What was it like to feel so much emotional pain that you wanted it to stop on any terms? Sometimes Christina felt that she knew the answer to that. This made her feel closer to Vanity, and in a strange way, she loved her even more now because of it.

Christina cast a wary glance at passersby. To the casual bystander, they must look like a couple of fast girls—too young, out too late, indulging in silly boyfriend dramas.

She watched Pippa shoot a concerned look to the street, where a monstrous Hummer limo had just crawled to a stop. A dark window zipped down, revealing a drunk and wild Shoshanna Biaggi.

"Pippa!" Max's sister slurred. "Get in . . . there's room . . . it's, like, a total VIP party . . ."

A bra got tossed out the window and landed in the gutter.

"That's not mine! I swear!" Shoshanna laughed uproariously.

"Can you believe how pissed out she is?" Pippa muttered under her breath.

"Should I go tell Max?" Christina wondered.

"No, I think he's seen enough for one night," Pippa answered, moving closer to the Hummer. She tried to get Shoshanna's attention. "You better go home and sober up—"

But before Pippa could get the directive out, one of the limo doors lurched open, and four male arms worked fast to pull her inside.

Christina's mouth dropped open in shock as everything happened in the space of an instant—Pippa's screaming, the slamming of the door, Shoshanna's piercing cackle, and the sight of the Hummer speeding away and disappearing into traffic.

At that moment, Christina's Sidekick II vibrated once more. No doubt the millionth call from her mother. She ignored it. Again. Then she just stood there for a long moment, trying to figure out what to do. Suddenly, it dawned on her to race back to Gino's for help. She took off. Before reaching the door, she noticed the Hummer stop in the middle of the street.

Christina watched Pippa swing out first, her body language daring *anybody* to mess with her. And then Pippa pulled Shoshanna out of the Hummer and dragged her by the arm until they reached the sidewalk.

By this point, the guys had made it outside and happened upon the scene, Max moving fast to intercept his sister, and Dante hanging back, looking despondent and distracted by his own thoughts.

Christina beamed a quick glance to her phone, then reluctantly called her mother.

"Where the hell *are* you? It's almost three o'clock in the morning!" Paulina raged after picking up on the first ring.

Right away Christina started to cry. "My friend was in a terrible accident."

"What friend?" Paulina hissed. "I've spoken to Wilmar and Eric half a dozen times tonight."

"Vanity," Christina wailed. "My friend . . . Vanity St. John."

Paulina sighed impatiently. "Stop being so overly dramatic, Christina. You barely know the girl."

"No, I do . . . I—I . . . love . . ." She was just on the brink of a confession.

"I want you home, Christina," Paulina cut in savagely. *"Now.* And I hope your night out was worth it, because it's going to be your last one for months." *Click.*

If tears gave away the secrets of feelings, then Christina's were fully exposed right now, a combination of the grief for Vanity and the shock of her mother's coldness.

All of a sudden she felt the envelopment of a strong embrace and realized that it was Dante. At that point, she really began to sob, letting all the emotion go. Her tears splashed down onto his shoulder as he wrapped her up with the warmth of his hug.

Christina was far and away, lost in the incredible sadness of what Vanity had done to herself. But deep down inside, she felt something close to joy, too. Because she realized that what her own mother denied her—compassion, comfort, a sense of family—could be discovered someplace else . . . with her new friends.

"It's going to be okay," Dante whispered.

Christina wanted so desperately to believe him. Still, she wondered if it really would be.

"I just had a few drinks!" Shoshanna roared belligerently, weaving back and forth as the words sputtered out. "Like that's a new thing!"

Max shut his eyes for a second, stealing himself to deal with the irritating situation before him. "Sho, this is beyond drunk. You can barely stand up."

"I'm fine!" Shoshanna insisted. She spread out her arms like airplane wings and attempted to prove it, failing miserably as she sang, "Because you're mine . . . I walk the line." Ultimately, she collapsed into a fit of laughter and fell down on the sidewalk.

Max took a quick step away, too furious to even look at her.

Pippa bent down to help.

"My brother's an asshole," Shoshanna slurred. "You can't really like him." She giggled. "You must just be after his money."

Max spun around.

Pippa abruptly stood up, leaving Shoshanna sprawled on the pavement. "She's *your* bloody sister. You help her."

Max stepped in and roughly pulled Shoshanna to her feet.

"Where's Yummy?" Shoshanna wondered.

Max turned to Pippa, a question in his eyes.

Pippa's eyes were flashing fire. "*Who* or *what* is a Yummy?"

"Her best friend," Max explained. "She's the same age."

Pippa shrugged. "I didn't see her. There were six guys in the Hummer. And Shoshanna."

Max grabbed his sister by both arms and shook her violently. "Do you realize how goddamn dangerous that is, Sho? To ride around with a group of guys you hardly know? When you're this drunk? Do you want to get gang raped? Do you want to end up like Natalee Holloway? Is that what you want?" He found his voice rising with each question, and by the end of the interrogation, he was shouting explosively.

"Let go!" Shoshanna screamed. "You're hurting me!"

Pippa tried to intervene. "Max, take it easy."

Max stopped and pulled Shoshanna to his chest, hugging her tightly, swaying backward and forward, side to side, gulping in great lungsful of air.

The raw grief hit hard. He was crying now, his whole body shuddering with emotion, his usually commanding voice small as he struggled to speak through the sobs. "I'm not going to let anything happen to you, Sho! Do you hear me? I'm not!"

He thought of Vanity and the sight of her being lifted from the wreckage. Oh God, it hurt. It hurt his heart. It hurt his soul. It hurt in places he never knew he had.

Max felt Pippa's hand on his shoulder. She was letting him know that she was there, and the gesture slowly tripped him back to equanimity.

Shoshanna was crying quietly.

Max withdrew his embrace, wiping away his tears and clearing his throat. He gave the area a circular glance. "Did Dante and Christina leave?"

Pippa nodded, moving fast to stop a subdued but still drunk Shoshanna from almost toppling over.

"I need to take care of something. Can you see that she gets home?"

Pippa gave him a strange look. "How? I rode with you."

Max shook his head. "Sorry. For one second there I

forgot that you're always bumming rides." He knew it was mean to say, but Pippa had seen him cry like a little bitch, and he was embarrassed. She needed to realize that the old Max was back.

Pippa glared at him. "I hope your trampy sister spews up her guts all over your Porsche!"

Mission accomplished.

"I'm taking a short walk," Max announced. "Don't let her fall in the gutter." He loped down the sidewalk and dialed J.J.'s number three or four times.

Finally, the stoner picked up, groggy as hell. "Max? What the hell? Don't you sleep? It's, like, after three."

"I can't get any sleep tonight. Why should you?"

J.J. groaned. "I'm baked, man. Can we talk later?"

"This won't take long. And you're always baked, so that's no excuse."

"Okay, okay. What's up? You got a deal for us on the Vanity vid?"

Max spoke in a clipped, authoritative, take-it-or-leave-it tone. "I've got a deal for *you,* so listen good, because I'm only going to say it once, you son of a bitch. I want the original and every available copy of that video. Walk away from this, and I'll set you up with a development exec at UPN. I know her well. She's the daughter of my father's agent. I can get you a talent holding deal at the network."

"I'll think about it."

"Thinking time's over. Do you want to be a model-slash-sleazebag or a model-slash-actor? The offer expires in five seconds."

There was a long beat of silence.

And then Max held his breath for the answer.

From: Vinnie

Ashley's sick.

Need you to dance tonight.

Big VIP coming in.

2:03 pm 9/29/05

chapter five

next onstage is a girl that nobody can seem to get enough of. She's blonde, she's barely legal—she's Star Baby!"

The DJ's velvety voice boomed from the loudspeakers and rang through the locker room, followed by the opening strains of "Slow" by Kylie Minogue. The crowd exploded with hungry applause, piercing whistles, and lewd catcalls.

The stupid bastards could wait.

Pursing her lips, Pippa gave her mouth a final once-over.

The Dior Bet on Pink gloss was shimmering to perfection. Carefully, she eased her feet into a brand-new pair of Christian Louboutin leopard-print platform sandals that, after sales tax, had set her back more than a thousand dollars.

Of course, the fact that the shoes were a work of art would be lost on the idiot men in the audience. After all, if they darkened the doors of Cheetah, then they only wanted to see tits, ass, and a tease of something more.

When Pippa finally walked onto the main stage, the impression lingered that she owned it lock, stock, and metal pole. Her immediate claim to fame among the patrons had been her superior diva bitch attitude. Oh, baby, she gave it to them good. And the salivating fools loved her for it. Why? Because they all wanted to believe that they had what it takes between their legs to bring her down a notch.

Ha! Men and their dicks. Never a smart combination. For them, that is. For Pippa, it was a brilliant pairing. Loads of cash were coming her way. In fact, she had shoe boxes full of money that she hadn't even counted yet.

Pippa swayed to the hypnotizing electronic beat, undulating her body just enough to drive them almost crazy. That's exactly where she held them off, too. *Almost* crazy. *Almost* touching her. *Almost* thinking they had a chance in bloody hell of finding out how she tasted and what she felt like. It was a delicate balancing act of subtle sexual torture.

And only two months since entering the world of exotic dancing, Pippa Keith had become a master of the game.

"Slow down and dance with me/Yeah, slow/Skip a beat and move with my body/Yeah, slow . . ."

The breathy voice of Kylie Minogue provided the soundtrack for Pippa's stage seduction as "Star Baby," the mysteriously young and oh-so-tender fantasy girl with the starfishlike scar a few inches underneath her left breast.

Pippa opened her legs and eased down into a standing squat position. The move transformed the entire alpha-hetero lot into a bunch of foaming-at-the-mouth loons. Her secret trick was to wet her thong before going on-stage. This gave the perverts a better peek at the little piece of heaven that would forever elude them.

When it came down to actual dancing, Pippa barely broke a sweat. Why bother? She could just stand up here reading the *Miami Herald* and still get fistfuls of dollars . . . as long as she did it half-naked.

Girls who gave it everything and more ended up injured. There were head traumas from hitting the pole, bruised bone points, stage burns, bunions, corns, spurs, sprained ankles, swollen knees, shin splints, lower back pain—the list went on and on. Who knew that taking off your clothes to music could have such occupational hazards? By comparison, playing in the NFL would be less damaging to the body.

The song ended. A throng of guys crowded the stage to throw money at her.

"Save me a private dance, Star Baby," a man with a goatee, a wedding ring, and at least fifty reasons to go on the South Beach Diet said.

"You're so beautiful!" another guy shouted. "How much to sit on my face?"

Pippa assassinated the pig with a haughty glare. "If you have to ask, dear, you *can't* afford it."

This triggered nervous laughter all around. Men. Put a hot, naked girl in front of them and their egos turned to eggshells.

Pippa loved it. She loved being in control of herself. She loved being in control of *them*. She loved the attention. She loved the cash. She loved the power. Oh God, yes, the *power*. On the stage, she ruled. And at the retail counters, she conquered.

"Excuse me, miss, but that particular bag is two thousand dollars." So warned the snooty bitch at the Chanel boutique in Bal Harbour Shops.

"Oh, is that all?" Pippa had responded innocently.

"Then I think I'll take the black one *and* the pink one. And be quick about it, darling. I'm pressed for time and still have stops to make at Louis Vuitton and Gucci."

Damage at the register—four grand. Look on the shopgirl's face—*priceless*. If Pippa wanted it, then Pippa bought it. Price tags didn't matter anymore. She was a total bling addict.

But the cash came with a cost. To make it meant working all the time. She never saw her friends or her mother anymore. Luckily, she could blame all of her time away on her new *job* as the assistant to an entertainment promoter. There was also the MACPA drama club. That was a great excuse as well. If they only knew. She was a permanent fixture at this vile place, a constant source of eye candy for these disgusting men.

Pippa left the stage and settled into a booth in the back corner to total up the appreciation. Three hundred dollars. Not bad for her first dance of the night.

A gaggle of men lurked nearby, gawking like schoolboys who'd found a peephole to the girls' locker room. The interest was in their eyes. The confidence to approach was not.

Finally, one of them stepped forward to prove that he had a pair. "Can I buy you a drink?"

She glanced up to do the man math. Married. Midthirties. Stopping in on his way home from work. Translation: A wallet with a Gold American Express that could take a beating. The smile that came with the question reached his eyes, revealing a certain kindness and decency that put Pippa instantly at ease.

As if on cue, the waitress swooped in to take the liquor

order. She knew to put water in Pippa's shot. She knew to boost the alcohol in the customer's. And she knew to keep the drinks coming.

"I'm Tommy."

"Little boys are named Tommy," Pippa teased gently. "You look like a man to me. Do you mind if I call you Tom?" She smiled.

He smiled back, swallowing hard, scarcely able to make direct eye contact.

Up close, Pippa was nothing short of flawless. This gave her a distinctive edge over most of the dancers at Cheetah. The other girls often broke the illusion of the ultimate fantasy with cheap makeup, discount perfume, bad Mystic tans, pole bruises, beat-up shoes, broken nails, tacky costumes, and the stench of cigarettes.

On a conscious level, men didn't necessarily take note of such things. After all, most guys would forgive a hairlip and missing teeth for a nice rack and a tight, shapely ass. But the allure of perfection could be a magical draw. It was the reason why Pippa took in double the money. Sometimes triple.

She used the most expensive cosmetics and booked time with top makeup artists to learn how to expertly apply the products herself. Spa-quality manicures and pedicures were a weekly ritual. Every piece of clothing that draped her body was from designer A-lines. None of this

Stella McCartney for H&M rubbish. Every pair of shoes that adorned her feet was cause for celebration—Manolo Blahnik, Jimmy Choo, Miu Miu.

But perhaps what separated her most from the pack was the way she smelled. Pippa owed it all to her new favorite fragrance, Love in White by Creed, a heady mixture of iris, white jasmine, magnolia, Bulgarian rose, daffodil, and other exotic notes. The impact was pure, sensual, intimate, and deliciously feminine. It had never failed to turn men into human ATM machines. It wouldn't fail now.

"I'd love a private dance."

"We could do that, Tom," Pippa said softly. "But we could also just sit here and talk."

"That sounds nice, too," he agreed.

Other dancers were eager to just grind a man raw and move on to the next horny subject. But Pippa knew better, thanks to shrewd coaching from Vinnie Rossetti, the manager of Cheetah. He proudly referred to her as "the club's new secret weapon."

This did nothing to endear Pippa to the rest of the girls. By nature, strippers could be a jaded group, regarding every new dancer as an enemy that would only take money out of their g-strings. So adding Pippa's exalted status as Vinnie's favorite pet to the mix made for a very tense environment.

But Pippa didn't care. She worked at Cheetah to make

money, not friends. Still, she hated to hear Vinnie openly brag to the other dancers that Star Baby was well on her way to becoming the club's number one girl. Though he hoped the threat would motivate them to do better, it only served to intensify their hatred toward Pippa.

The ringleader of the hostility was an older dancer who went by the oh-so-subtle stage name Hellcat. She was a tall, hardened blonde with big fake breasts, multiple piercings, and more body art than Angelina Jolie. With Pippa being the lone exception, all the dancers kissed her ass and submitted to her controlling ways. She ruled over them like an underground empress.

Nothing stopped Hellcat from racking up dollars and private dances. She was a steel-nerved, borderline psychotic, money-making machine. One night she caught a nipple piercing in her hair during a head flip. The jewelry ripped out, and blood poured from the wound. But Hellcat just let it gush, song after song, spreading the blood all over her body like a satanic ritualist while she went about the business of providing lap dances.

Despite the firsthand evidence that she was indeed a warm-blooded creature, Pippa still felt certain that the woman had ice water running through her veins. Oh, yes. Hellcat was the coldest bitch ever. And if Pippa could survive her, then she could survive *anything*.

But right now she had to survive the act of pretending

that *Tom* was interesting. That would be one tough order, too. Because the guy was a big fat bore. Whenever in crisis, though, Pippa just channeled the voice of Vinnie inside her head.

"Talk to your customer," he'd advised on her first night. "Really talk to him. Ask about his job and fake it like you actually give a damn. Say his name a lot and give him compliments. The average guy would rather sit down and talk to a beautiful woman who puts him on a pedestal than get a quick and dirty dance. Think about it. He's probably going home to an overweight wife who doesn't give head, complains about everything, and thinks he's a lazy sack of shit. Trust me. It'll be the easiest money you've ever made."

And it was.

"What kind of work are you in, Tom?" Pippa asked.

"I sell cars."

"Oh, wow," Pippa cooed convincingly. "I *love* cars."

"I sell BMWs," Tom said proudly.

"Really? That's hot." Oh God, she was beyond bored. Different loser guy, same stupid shit.

He beamed.

"I bet you know a lot about next year's models. Will you buy me another drink and tell me all about them?" It was all she could do to sound like she cared even a little bit.

"Sure." Before he had a chance to signal the waitress, she was there with another round.

And so it went. Tom drank single malt scotch and talked BMWs. Pippa drank water that was supposed to be vodka and hung on his every word. By the end of the charade, Cheetah charged Tom's credit card for ten drinks and five private dances. Then Vinnie put the wasted salad dodger in a cab and sent him home.

Reluctantly, Pippa slipped back into the locker room to freshen up. She hated being in this backstage hell swamped with bright fluorescent lighting. It reeked of sweat, drugstore perfume, and cigarettes.

Girls in various stages of nakedness held court near their assigned changing areas. Each space looked like a landfill of makeup cases, costume racks, and caffeine-charged drinks.

The moment Pippa stepped inside, she knew that something was very wrong. A conspiratorial silence boomed. Secret glances went back and forth among the girls. Bitchy giggles were shared. Nobody gave Pippa eye contact except Hellcat, who was staring daggers straight through her.

Pippa approached her station, only to find that it was empty. "Where's my stuff?" she demanded of no one in particular.

"Vinnie moved it," Hellcat announced. "He gave you Ashley's spot."

Pippa was genuinely stunned. Everybody considered

that station coveted real estate because it was positioned closest to the bathroom. In the demimonde of Cheetah stripper culture, it signified that you were the top girl, which Ashley was. Or had been. "She's not coming back?"

LaTonya, one of the few African-American dancers at Cheetah and intermittently a friendly presence to Pippa, slammed the door to her locker and started toward the exit, spilling out of a very naughty nurse's uniform. "She can call in sick with that fake-ass cough all she wants. I heard the bitch is dancing at Scores." And with that, LaTonya disappeared as the opening guitar licks of Mötley Crüe's "Dr. Feelgood" growled from the sound system.

Pippa rolled her eyes. She had nothing to do with Ashley defecting to a rival club. She had nothing to do with Vinnie giving her Ashley's space, either. As if any of this mattered. Sack it! She was *so* above skuzzy stripper drama.

She pushed onward to her new locker, then stopped suddenly, letting out an audible gasp. Scrawled in ugly blood-red lipstick across her dressing mirror were the words "STAR CUNT."

"Congratulations, *Star Baby,*" Hellcat trilled, her raspy smoker's voice dripping with venom. "Is something the matter? Did I spell your name wrong?" She laughed at her own joke.

A chorus of other girls joined in, relishing the vicious fun at Pippa's expense.

"What's going on here?" Vinnie demanded.

Pippa spun quickly, startled by his sudden presence in the locker room.

Sizing up the situation, he took in the defaced mirror and glared at Hellcat. "You have time for bullshit like this? No wonder your earnings are off this week."

Hellcat betrayed no reaction.

Vinnie gave the hardcore dancer a relentless face-to-face stare, until his gaze traveled down to zero in on her crotch. "When's the last time you had a decent wax?"

A few girls burst into titters.

Before Hellcat could answer the question, Vinnie said, "I think I've got a rake in the back of my truck if you need to smooth that out before you go onstage."

The titters upgraded to uncontrollable guffaws.

Hellcat's face went red hot with the fire of humiliation.

Vinnie turned to Pippa. "You've got a VIP waiting upstairs. Take real good care of him. I know you've got what it takes." He gave her an avuncular pat on the ass and started to leave. Abruptly, he stopped to issue Hellcat another withering look. "Clean that crap off the mirror. And get this through that slit you call a brain—*nobody* messes with Star Baby. She's the new golden pussy around here. Learn to live with that. Or get the fuck out." His voice rose to address the entire locker room. "The same goes for all of you bitches!" And then Vinnie stormed out, leaving a deafening silence in his wake.

Pippa shut her eyes. Backstage life at Cheetah had been hard enough. It was about to get that much harder. She tried to shake off the anxiety with a series of slow, deep breaths as she applied fresh gloss to her lips, fluffed out her hair, and changed into a lace-trimmed seersucker bra and panties set by Prada.

Feeling her energy level dip, she popped open a lukewarm can of Red Bull and chased it down faster than a sorority girl funneling beer at a tailgate party. She had to dazzle the VIP and seduce him into ordering a jeroboam of Piper-Heidsieck Cuveé Brut champagne. She had to read three chapters of Harper Lee's *To Kill a Mockingbird* for English class. And she had to avoid that menace to pole-dancing society who called herself Hellcat.

Welcome to high school life, Pippa Keith style.

And the deepest, darkest truth—she hated it, this new life. The lies to her mother, the lies to her friends, the hungry stares from the disgusting men, the vicious looks from the other girls—day in and day out, the grind was beginning to take its toll.

Pippa slipped off her Christian Louboutins and eased into an equally expensive pair of peep-toe wedges by Chanel. She was just adjusting the last strap when someone slammed into her shoulder.

The force sent Pippa stumbling, knocking her against a chair and down to the ground. At the last possible moment, she splayed out her hands just wide and high enough to break the fall and avoid damaging a nail.

Hellcat towered over her, pulling the trigger on a red stiletto switchblade, then quickly folded the business end back to its original closed position. "Careful, Star Cunt. I'd hate for a clumsy girl like you to fall on something sharp one day."

For a moment, Pippa lay there, paralyzed, unable to take her eyes off the huge python tattoo slithering on Hellcat's back flesh as the tough-as-nails bitch walked away.

Nobody made a move to help Pippa to her feet. She scrambled up on her own, put herself back together, and stalked out. It was a brave front that belied the chill-inducing terror she felt inside.

Ascending the flight of stairs that led up to the Lair, Pippa came to the frightening realization that Vinnie could only protect her so much. Maybe the time had come to quit. Granted, the money was fantastic, but being alive was far more precious. If Vanity St. John's car accident had taught Pippa any lesson over the last two months, then it was that.

Even now, the group, the once fabulous five, was still adjusting to life without her. Vanity's absence had significant and far-reaching influence. Her role had been like that of the sun, a giant, glowing star for other planets to orbit around.

Everything was changing. Every*one* was changing. Or maybe just Pippa was. Vinnie scheduled her to dance on most nights, which meant there was little time to hang out with Max, Dante, and Christina. She missed it—the dinners, the club outings, the late-night talks before sleep. But whenever she made noises about cutting back, Vinnie made noises about a VIP that would make every night at Cheetah worthwhile. She wondered if tonight's client might finally live up to the hype.

With each step, the door to the Lair loomed closer and closer. Private time with VIPs could be quite the tightwire act. Sometimes they expected more than Pippa was willing to do. But no matter how much they offered to pay, she felt no temptation to accommodate them. The distance from stripper to whore was a short one, and Pippa vowed never to make that trip.

Besides, Vinnie cautioned her that the day she went too far with a customer was the day she would have to start working harder for the money. Being unattainable kept the men coming back again and again. Often, Pippa could command more than one hundred dollars a song and not even touch a guy. It was amazing how much mileage she could get out of breathing in a man's ear. That alone could kill most of them. Oh, yes. Some sweet wind to the lobe always got them by the short and curlies!

Of course, VIPs could also be total spazmos. Like the CEO who paid big bucks for Pippa to listen to a stroke-by-stroke account of his latest golf game. Or the local news anchor who wanted to brush her hair while she read aloud from the Henry James novel *The Portrait of a Lady.* Very weird. But such easy cash that Pippa felt like she was robbing the silly blokes.

Quietly, she opened the door to the Lair and slipped inside. Percolating on a Bose iPod SoundDock was "One of These Nights" by the Eagles. The room was small, boldly decorated with red walls, zebra-print carpet, an oversize leopard-print sofa, and a rectangular, white-lacquered coffee table, atop which sat a silver champagne bucket icing down an unopened bottle of Cristal. Hmm. He was already a big bar spender. This interlude should pay out big.

The unidentified VIP, shadowed by the dim lighting from the Noguchi paper lanterns, sat kicked back on the sofa. "I've been waiting for this moment, Star Baby," he said in a rich baritone voice that exuded wealth, charisma, confidence, and sex appeal. "I've had you on my radar for weeks."

Pippa stepped forward. The shadows cleared. What she saw next knocked the breath from her body. Sitting there with a rakish grin on his handsome face was Max Biaggi.

Superstar.

Action hero.

Movie legend.

And father of her best mate.

From: Mom

I have another protest rally tonight plus a fund-raiser.
Don't forget to eat dinner!

11:54 am 10/01/05

chapter six

Christina toyed with the edamame and managed to get down most of the carrot-and-dill soup. MACPA lunches had gone the haute cuisine route, and the food was delicious. But she just wasn't that hungry.

A parent committee led by a cookbook editor and the wife of a Miami restaurant baron had started a nutritional movement that resulted in a new slate of cosmopolitan and healthy gourmet selections. For a salad, there was no longer a ranch dressing option. Tomato vinaigrette ruled the day.

Max wolfed down his cilantro-and-jalapeno–marinated tofu. "Some days I miss the old crap," he said. "I mean, Jesus, we're seventeen. Aren't we *supposed* to survive on greasy pizza, Mountain Dew, and hot dogs that bounce like rubber?"

Christina cracked a smile. "Haven't you heard? We want the kind of food that will go with our Louis Vuitton bags."

Max shook his head. "Bling addiction is everywhere. It's like a disease."

Christina laughed. "Says the guy with a Rolex Submariner strapped to his wrist. What's wrong? Can't you tell time with a Casio digital?"

"I'm not talking about me. I've got an image to maintain. I'm supposed to have this shit. My father's a movie star, remember? Anything less is disrespecting the family brand. I can't walk around looking like a Wal-Mart cart."

"So it's just *other* people who have a bling addiction," Christina surmised, her voice teasing. "Your fashion choices are . . . practical."

"Exactly," Max agreed, picking up on her sarcasm but choosing to ignore it. "I heard about a guy who maxed out a credit card just so he could have the same outfit Kanye West wore to the MTV VMAs. The dude makes minimum wage at a *Smoothie King.* It's sick. And girls are just as bad, if not worse. But they don't have to mash carob and bananas into a blender for some fat ass. If they want a new purse and can't afford one, all they have to do is blow a couple of guys. Abracadabra—instant Prada. I'm telling you. It's a sick world out there."

"Believe me, I know how sick it is," Christina said, her thoughts fast-forwarding to tonight's newscasts and tomorrow's morning paper.

What was the old journalism axiom? Oh, yes. If it bleeds, it leads. Well, Christina had coined another one: If it hates, it rates.

Paulina Perez had become a polarizing yet high-profile media opportunist with her quest to shut down every school-sponsored gay/straight student alliance in Miami.

Christina tried to stay lost in her own world, to pretend that none of it was happening. But how could she ignore her own mother shrieking on television about teenagers being brainwashed by a liberal society into living a "depraved homosexual lifestyle."

Beyond the endless embarrassment, Christina's biggest problem with the campaign was that, politically at least, it happened to be working in her mother's favor. This early-bird strategy to get a head start on next year's Senate seat race actually had her *leading* in the current polls, an achievement in no small measure owed to the support of African-American and Hispanic voters.

It amazed Christina how these groups could be manipulated into choosing candidates based on moral issue crusades that didn't impact their daily lives. What about health care, job growth, and the environment? Christina didn't even know her mother's position on those topics.

But one thing was certain. Paulina didn't think that Mike and Steve should be allowed to go to their high school prom as a couple. Now there's a platform. Cast those ballots and send the woman to Washington. God! The voting public didn't have a clue. Christina wasn't even eligible yet, and she could see through the bullshit. So why were people thirty and older so absolutely stupid?

"If I didn't know any better, Jap, I'd say you were sounding a bit cynical," Max observed, grinning as he finished off a liter-size bottle of Evian. He knew how much that nickname—an offensive nod to her love of *manga*—got on her nerves. "I thought you were the sensitive artist type who wanted to save the whales, the trees, and all the poor children."

"Maybe I'm becoming wise to the world," Christina told him.

"Don't do that," Max said. "I like the girl who can't stay out past eleven and always has her face buried in a comic book or a sketch pad. It's about the only thing around here that's still normal." A forlorn expression skated across his face.

Lately it had just been the two of them during lunch, sprawled out in the third-floor hallway, their backs propped against the blue lockers as they sampled the exotic new menu.

Vanity had been out of their lives since the summer,

Dante never seemed to leave MACPA's new recording studio, and Pippa was always busy with rehearsals for her lead performance in the school's winter production of *Sweet Charity.*

Christina could hardly bring herself to think about Vanity without getting emotional. Even two months after the accident. It still seemed like yesterday. Yet it seemed like a lifetime ago, too. She sought solace in the creation of her own *manga, Harmony Girl,* whose title character was based on Vanity. At once, the creative outlet helped Christina celebrate and reconcile her feelings.

It was strange, though. Everything in the real world drove home the point that any dream she harbored for a romance with Vanity would never happen. Yet working on the fantasy comic itself made her fall in love with the girl as if for the very first time.

"Are you up for poker tonight?" Max asked.

"What's the buy-in?"

He grinned. "Only two grand."

"Is that all?" Dante asked, swooping down with a double-size Rockstar Energy Cola. "Sounds like a bingo game, bitch."

"Dude!" Max exclaimed, obviously surprised to see him. "Does that mean you're in?"

"What's the status of my Biaggi house account?" Dante asked.

"Nonexistent," Max cracked.

"Then I'm out," Dante said.

Max turned to Christina. "What about you, Jap?"

Two thousand dollars? What am I supposed to do—raid my mother's campaign coffers?

Max laughed. "That's not a bad idea. You'd certainly be putting the money to better use. Even if you lost it all in the first hand."

Christina smiled. "Well, you're probably right, but count me out anyway. Why so high?"

"Some frats from the University of Miami want to play like they've got big dicks and fat wallets." Max shrugged. "But I'll castrate the losers and make them learn the hard way that they don't have point money. Just another Monday night on Star Island."

"What's point money?" Christina asked.

"As in fifty-one-point-two." One beat. "Mil." Another beat. "That's the amount in my trust fund."

"Notice he's not talking about the size of his dick," Dante teased.

Christina rolled her eyes. "Only because that was *yesterday's* lunch topic."

Dante laughed.

"I'll be happy to recap since you're present and accounted for today," Max said, smirking. "I know what a size queen you are."

"And how would you know that exactly?" Pippa wondered out loud as she approached her locker.

Dante stood up. "He thinks I'm gay because I like Coldplay."

Pippa giggled, then bent down to snatch one of Christina's edamame.

"It's a sign, dude," Max said. "That's all I'm saying. Okay, last chance. Does anybody want in on this game tonight?"

"What game?" Pippa asked.

Max proudly rattled off the details. "Poker. The Biaggi basement. Two-thousand-dollar minimum."

"Do you know boys who actually bet that much, or is this just an excuse for you to sit around and play with your skin flutes?" Pippa flashed a smile, then disappeared as she rushed down the hall.

"I think I've been insulted," Max murmured.

"Can't keep anything from you," Dante cracked, giving Max a patronizing pat on the shoulder as he walked away.

Max rose up on his haunches and slung his beaten-but-still-beautiful Tod's backpack over his shoulder. "Okay, Jap, I hate to leave you sitting here all alone like the loser you used to be, but I really must go." He worked his brow up and down in a lewd manner. *"Judith* wants to talk to me about college."

"Judith as in Judith Dalton, the school counselor?"

Max stood to his full height. "We're on a first-name basis now. She wants me. But I'm holding out on the sex until just before she writes my letter of rec. I want her to still be panting from a Maxgasm for that assignment."

Christina laughed. "She's married!"

"Have you seen her husband?" Max asked. "He wears one of those yellow silicone LIVESTRONG bracelets. And he drives a hybrid. Major tool."

"You're so wrong!" Christina yelled with amusement as Max took off. She was picking at what remained of her edamame when someone approached her.

"Excuse me, I'm new here, and I obviously don't get it. What's up with everybody eating in the hall?"

Christina looked up to see a short, edgy Asian girl. She was seriously punked out—hot pink hair, brow, nose, and tongue piercings, and raccoon-style eye makeup. In her flashy yellow Donna tank by Betsey Johnson, plaid mini, fishnet hose riddled with holes, rips, and runs, and military-style boots, she looked camera ready to lead an anti-anything revolution.

"They're using the cafeteria as an extra rehearsal space for a big show," Christina explained. "It's only temporary." She smiled kindly.

The girl took a ravenous bite out of her Greek stuffed grape leaf wrap. Some of the rice filling spilled onto the floor. She either didn't notice or didn't care because she just left it there. "Do you mind if I sit?" She gestured to the same spot Max had just vacated.

Christina nodded. "Go ahead."

The girl crashed down. "So what are the kids like at this school? Do they suck, or are most of them okay?"

Christina was taken aback by her aggression. "It varies, I guess."

With her slight frame, the girl looked too young to be in high school and too small for most of the rides at Disney World. "I just moved from San Francisco. I hope there are some hot dykes here."

Christina was speechless.

"Chill out. I'm not hitting on you. If I was, you'd know it because I'd have my tongue down your throat." She laughed a throaty laugh. "I'm Keiko. Keiko Naka-mura."

"Christina Perez." Beads of sweat prickled under her arms, her cheeks went hot, and she found herself struggling for breath. Something about the girl left Christina feeling vulnerable and exposed, as if Keiko had the power to take one good look at her and instantly discover her secret.

"Perez," Keiko repeated thoughtfully. "Are you related to that psycho bitch who's running for senator?"

"Guilty by birth," Christina admitted.

"For real?" Keiko demanded, not quite believing her.

Christina nodded severely.

"You know that you're going to be in therapy for years and years, right?"

"Oh, I think I'll be institutionalized first," Christina cracked.

Keiko laughed again. She threw back her head and let the severe geometry of her choppy hairstyle fly this way and that. "So what's her deal? Was your dad, like, a closet fag or something? Is that why she has a broomstick up her ass about gays?"

"My father died in a car accident," Christina snapped. "And he wasn't gay."

"*Sorry,*" Keiko answered. "I didn't mean anything." But it was more of a scolding for Christina's sharp reaction than an actual apology.

A strained silence hung between them.

Finally, Keiko broke it. "Your mom would freak if she knew what we did at my old school."

Christina looked at her with guarded interest.

"You know how it's usually against the rules to make out in school, but guys and girls do it anyway with no problem?"

Christina nodded.

"Well, one day I was kissing my girlfriend at her locker, and we got suspended for that. So we staged a kiss-off on the front lawn. Every queer and dyke in the school left their classes and marched out there to kiss. They put pictures in the newspaper and everything. We even got on television. It was awesome."

Christina just sat there, mesmerized, and more than a little envious. Keiko seemed to be living with such freedom about who she was—openly and unapologetically.

"Do you have a girlfriend?"

Christina drew back, thunderstruck by the question. It was the first time anyone had ever asked or assumed anything about her sexuality. The answer rolling around in her mind was no, but the words that came spilling out of her mouth were, "How did you know?"

Keiko grinned. "I can just tell. Take me to the baby wing at a hospital. I'll point out every newborn gay boy and girl and won't be wrong about any of them."

Christina experienced a strange sensation. She took a soul-searching moment to identify the feeling. It was relief. For the first time in her life, she had been completely honest with another person. And instead of being afraid, she felt emboldened.

Keiko beamed a mischievous smile. "I think we could get into a lot of trouble together."

Now Christina was frightened. Because she liked the sound of that. She liked the sound of that very much indeed.

From: Mimi

Whatever happened to Vanity St. John?

9:27 am 10/31/05

chapter seven

*W*hatever happened to Vanity St. John?

Vanity read the text and mulled over half a dozen bitchy responses, ultimately tapping out none of them. Did it even matter anymore?

Three months had passed since the accident. And in the world of celebrity PR where one is famous for being famous and not famous for possessing any demonstrative talent, three months might as well be three years.

Whatever happened to Vanity St. John?

Did the fawning public really want to know the gory details of her miserable life? No. Would the hacks for *People, Us Weekly,* and *Star* actually scribble down a story that had nothing to do with designer clothes, dating, or the alleged ongoing feuds with Lindsay Lohan and Katee K? Hell no.

Mimi Blair might be a clever pitch-and-spin girl, but she was hardly Zatanna, Mistress of Magic. There was no sexy hook to the purgatory that had become Vanity's isolated existence.

When her Mercedes crashed into the fuel tanker, the difference between serious injury and certain death had been inches apart. She narrowly avoided going out in an explosive fireball blaze. Instead, she got crushed like a soda can, cracking several ribs and shattering her tibia in what the doctors called a triple displaced spiral.

You're lucky to be alive.

That's what the first responders on the scene had told her. But she didn't feel lucky then. And she didn't feel lucky now.

There was a metal plate in her leg. There were eight screws holding it down. Usually, one surgery was enough to get the job done. But in her case, complications had required four.

The doctors ordered twelve weeks of bed rest, clearing her only to use the bathroom. So she just lay there day after day, crying uncontrollably from the agony, the muscle cramps, and the spasms.

Her reliance on painkillers became a concern early into her so-called recovery. They said she was displaying classic symptoms of addiction and took away her precious Vicodin, immediately switching her to Ultram, an arthritis medication. It helped with the pain, so she endured the ugly side effects—swelling, skin rashes, and constant dry mouth.

It was slow torture. She suffered diarrhea from the strong antibiotics prescribed to prevent bone infection, and beyond that she suffered constipation from the calcium tabs that they told her to chew like candy.

The endless hours stretched to endless days, the endless weeks to endless months. Her depression seemed bottomless, and Vanity plunged deeper and deeper into it, refusing visits from friends and ignoring their calls. Yet when the odd moment of wanting company materialized, she bitterly resented them for not being there. Soon she grew to hate Max, Christina, Pippa, and Dante more than she grew to miss them. She knew this was irrational and unfair. But these were her feelings.

Vanity's life became a cocoon of sleep, television, and more sleep, the monotony broken only by regular visits from Walter "Steak" Williams, the physical therapist who pushed her through a brutal regimen of painful exercises designed to accelerate her recovery.

Steak was big, black, loud, and unrelenting. Vanity loathed the therapy but adored him. He made her laugh with stories about his crazy romantic life, encouraged her to push harder, declared "Stickwitu" by the Pussycat Dolls as their special song, and assured her that one day soon she would be vamping around like a contestant on *America's Next Top Model.*

But that was Steak being an eternal optimist. Regular X-rays and radiographs indicated slow healing to the bone. That meant another surgery to undo one of the screws on the internal fixator. It also meant a round of low-frequency ultrasound treatments and another month of no weight-bearing movement on the leg. At this rate, walking on her own by New Year's Eve would be a medical miracle.

Simon St. John pretended to be a father. When he was in town, he always checked on her before leaving for the office and then again as soon as he returned home. Vanity could usually predict his appearances and feigned sleep to avoid interaction.

Isis St. John pretended to be a mother. She called once and tried to relate to her daughter by telling a rambling story about the time she sprained her ankle at a disco in Ibiza. Then she announced her "conversion to Kaballahism" and promised to send a gift. A few weeks later, a red string bracelet arrived via airmail from Nice, France. The attached note said that wearing it would protect her from the evil eye. Vanity tossed the stupid thing into the garbage.

If there was any light to the darkness at all, then it was

Vanity's growing affection for Mercedes and Gunnar, her younger siblings. The twins staged elaborate shows and performed them in the doorway of Vanity's bedroom, then ran away squealing with laughter. Their antics were a welcome respite from the idiots on *Laguna Beach,* which Vanity watched with religious fervor.

Another pleasant surprise had been Vanity's sudden tolerance for Lala. The twins' nanny brooked no argument about her extra duties as nursemaid. She nagged Vanity to keep herself properly hydrated and ferried her back and forth to the hospital for tests and checkups.

Today she was taking her to see Dr. Parker. In the aftermath of the accident, the surgeries and strict bed rest had dimmed Vanity's session frequency to once a month at best, so she looked forward to these hours with something close to desperation. Lala would wheel her into the waiting room, then disappear to the Lincoln Road Mall until Vanity called to say she was ready.

Even with the awkwardness of being restricted to a wheelchair, Dr. Parker's customary hug felt so nurturing as to be medicinal. Vanity didn't want it to end, and when the embrace was broken, she started to cry.

"It's hard, isn't it?" Dr. Parker asked softly, offering Vanity a few tissues.

She nodded and dabbed at the tears in her eyes. God, she felt so dumb. "I'm sorry. You must think I'm pathetic."

"Of course not." Dr. Parker allowed Vanity a moment to settle down. "How are you?"

Vanity went through the last few weeks of leg trauma in great detail. This made her feel like the old woman down the street who holds neighbors hostage as she discusses every ache and pain. It was all that Vanity knew, though. Her world had become that small.

At first, Dr. Parker listened patiently. But finally, she chose to break in. "Is this really helping, Vanity?"

"Why? Am I boring you?"

"No. You're avoiding me."

"I'm here, aren't I?"

"It's not enough to just show up. You have to be present and willing to do the emotional work."

Vanity inspected her nails, purposefully avoiding Dr. Parker's stare. There were no free passes in this room, even when you arrived in a wheelchair.

"Let's move beyond the physical. The doctors anticipate a full recovery. Frankly, that's all the information I need about your leg. I'm more concerned about what's going on inside of you."

Vanity decided to come out with it. "I secretly dread the idea of walking again."

"Why?"

"Because I don't feel like I've changed. I'm the same person who was driving too fast with her eyes closed three months ago. It scares me that coming so close to death and going through all of this hasn't made any difference. I'm still stuck. The only change is that I now know that I really don't want to kill myself." She shrugged helplessly. "But I don't necessarily want to live, either."

Dr. Parker leaned forward. "That's a very brave thing to admit. I'm glad to hear you say it."

Vanity gave her a quizzical look. "You're glad that I'm a zombie?"

Dr. Parker smiled. "No. I'm glad that you have the depth of self-awareness to recognize these feelings. Some people go through their entire lives with that kind of ambivalence, but they have no idea how to articulate it. You just did." She reached out and clasped Vanity's hand. "This is a huge breakthrough." And then she released it, settling back into her chair. "Let's keep going. I want to hear more about your reluctance to get back to your routine."

Vanity sighed deeply. "I don't know . . . maybe it's because I don't know what I'm getting back to exactly. All of my friends have something. Dante has his music, Christina's an artist, Pippa's a dancer, and Max . . . well, he just plays poker and plans parties, but at least it's *something.*"

"An engrossing passion," Dr. Parker clarified.

"Yeah." Vanity nodded. *"I don't have that.* I complain

about being famous. I hate the way people only seem to be interested in what I'm wearing, how much weight I've gained or lost, or whatever. But then I have to think, you know . . . is there anything else to me?"

"Only you have the power to determine that."

Vanity shook her head vigorously. "I don't think I'm hardwired that way. My first instinct is to worry about my looks. It's been that way all of my life. Nobody has ever told me that I'm smart or funny or good at anything other than . . . *this.*" She swept both hands down her torso. "The package—my face, my hair, my body." She paused a moment to collect her thoughts. "Lately, I've been thinking a lot about the sex video that J.J. had. When I first heard about it, I was so upset. You know? I was *mad.* All I could think about was how humiliating it would be. But now part of me *wishes* it would come out." She managed half a laugh. "Isn't that crazy?"

Dr. Parker didn't answer.

"You see, I know that I was hot then," Vanity went on. "I wasn't puffy like I am now from this goddamn Ultram. I was tan. You could bounce a quarter off my abs *and* my ass. I realize that makes me an object . . . but that's the only attention I know." She let out a long frustrated breath. "Am I making any sense?"

"Does it make sense to you?"

"Yes."

"Then we're doing good work here." Dr. Parker tilted her head curiously. "Tell me what you *don't* want. If you could say no to one thing, what would it be?"

Vanity considered the question carefully. "Sex."

Dr. Parker revealed nothing. "Go on."

"I've had a lot of it, but I've never wanted it. Don't get me wrong. I've never been the victim of a rape. I always went along *voluntarily* . . . but it never had anything to do with what I wanted or desired or fantasized about. It was just a performance. You know, a way to get attention. Even with Dante, I can't say that I actually wanted it. I was performing. I rescued him on the beach, and I took him for a ride on my boat, and I gave him a blow job in the middle of the ocean. The whole time I was thinking, *This is so hot for him that he's going to keep coming back.* I'm not sure if I've ever been fully aroused. I mean, I don't even see the point in masturbating. I get the idea of doing it in front of a guy, because he would be turned on. But I never think about doing it for myself. You know, just to feel good."

Dr. Parker nodded intently. "Female desire is very complicated, and just because you're having sex doesn't mean that you're expressing your sexuality."

Vanity grinned. "So does that mean I'm still a virgin?"

Dr. Parker laughed. "Oh, I'd say that ship has sailed. At least in the traditional sense." She gave Vanity a long, penetrating look. "Let's talk about your friends. Do you miss them?"

"It's difficult to say."

"Why?"

"Because I'm not sure that I know how to relate to them anymore. That's why I don't answer the phone. That's why I tell Lala to tell them I'm sleeping if they happen to drop by."

"But how will you know for sure if all you do is shut them out?"

"I used to be the It girl, Dr. Parker. Everything about me was larger than life. Now I'm just this . . . depressed girl. My life barely extends beyond my bedroom."

"But their lives are still rich and active. That's the real problem, isn't it?"

Vanity cast a downward glance, shamefully avoiding eye contact. "I resent them, Dr. Parker. I resent them for everything—for walking, for being happy, for trying too hard to reach out, for not trying hard enough. At one point I felt indebted to Max because he negotiated with J.J. to get rid of the sex tape. But now I feel like he cheated me out of something."

"In what way?"

"That video is an example of the girl that I was. I want to be her again. I just don't know how."

From: Max

It's Thanksgiving night, and I'm thankful for the bottle
of Hennessy in one hand and the bottle of Hpnotiq in
the other. What about u?

10:14 pm 11/24/05

chapter eight

I don't pop my cork for every guy I see . . ."

Star Baby had taken the holiday off. Tonight Pippa was Charity Hope Valentine.

Sexy Charity. Hot Charity. *Sweet Charity.*

"Hey big spender/Spend a little time with me . . ."

She ran through the intricate choreography like a Broadway darling. Step-turn-spin-kick. She belted out the sassy lyrics like a stage diva.

"What is this shit?" a fat loser shouted. "I feel like I'm watching 'American Idol'! Just show us your tits, baby!"

Customers who showed up on Thanksgiving made for a tough crowd. Men *without* a family at home got drunk because they were lonely and unsatisfied. Men *with* a family at home got drunk for the same reasons.

Oh, sack it! Pippa ripped open her blouse and gave the swamp donkeys exactly what they wanted. It was bloody amazing what boobs were capable of.

Every molecule of restlessness evaporated from the room. At the mere sight of two pouting and ambitious cones of female flesh, their hopelessly dull lives were instantly steamed up.

The music stopped.

Pippa approached the lip of the stage to collect the cash. After every dance, she'd grown quite accustomed to money raining down. But tonight it only drizzled.

The tepid response infuriated her. Strip club trolls were so gross. The vile pigs just sat there—drinking, smoking, eyeballing, groping, yelling. How could she expect such a sorry lot to appreciate a *real* song and dance? Chances of that were about as likely as these pervs watching a porno movie to enjoy the plot.

Pippa's new-girl novelty at Cheetah seemed to be fading a bit. The diehards wanted her to be more like the other dancers. Ha! Keep dreaming, spunk monsters. She had no intention of hitting the stage in a neon green tube top and whipping her hair around so dramatically that she developed a bulged disc. Pippa happened to be the only girl in the club who didn't have neck problems. And she planned on keeping it that way.

So what if her big number from *Sweet Charity* didn't

give the assholes a stiffy. At least she got some practice in *and* earned enough to buy a new pair of Fendi sunglasses. Not her best night. But still productive.

MACPA's winter spectacular was set for early February. Pippa burned with anticipation for her chance to bring the audience to their feet with her two rip-roaring showstoppers, "Big Spender" and "If My Friends Could See Me Now."

Oh God, she loved being part of a big-budget musical. And snaring the *lead* in her first year? Loads cool. Luckily, the theater department had a new head, Bill Booker. As far as he was concerned, none of the students deserved to be in the program until they proved otherwise. The man was a swishy, bitchy black fag who insisted that everyone call him Miss Bill. He worked his cast and technical crew like cattle, rarely dishing out praise.

Pippa maintained a constant state of amazement over the grand scale of a senior MACPA production. This was no school play with PTA mums knitting homemade costumes at the last minute. MACPA's state-of-the-art auditorium seated nine hundred, and the backstage capabilities included closed-circuit television monitors, fly rails for raising and lowering large set pieces, and a scene shop with its own loading bay.

"You are *professionals*," Miss Bill hissed at the beginning and end of every rehearsal. "I expect you to be serious, confident, and daring on this stage."

At first, everybody hated him. But as opening night loomed closer and closer, they loved him silly. Miss Bill ran a torture chamber, but the end result was a cast blossoming under his pressure, having the time of their lives, and pushing themselves to the peaks of their talents.

"Lady P, I need you to *project*!" Miss Bill had snapped this at least a million times. "Don't rely on the microphone, girlfriend. What if it's not working? They paid twenty-five dollars for those seats in the balcony, and they want to hear Miss Charity sing!"

And so she practiced *projecting*. Anywhere she could. Miss Bill would absolutely die if he knew that her dedication extended to giving it a go at Cheetah, singing for her supper in a g-string to a bunch of horny bastards still sleepy from their turkey dinners.

But Pippa was prepared to do whatever it took, because the stakes were high. Miss Bill had just informed the cast that the show was in the running for a weeklong slot at a professional summer stock amphitheater in upstate New York.

The exhausting *Sweet Charity* gauntlet had almost—but not quite—crowded out Pippa's obsession with money and shopping. She loved playing Charity Hope Valentine, the taxi dancer with the heart of gold who was torn between a handsome movie star and an ordinary desk worker.

The show was based on a Fellini film called *Nights of Cabiria,* and Miss Bill had reworked the book and music to give it a modern edge, transforming Charity's movie star love interest into a Jay-Z mogul type and the accountant she meets in an elevator into a FedEx courier. Beyond that, Miss Bill had spiced up the musical arrangements with funk flourishes, especially in the final number, when the entire cast performed the Missy Elliott version of "Big Spender," complete with Ciara-inspired hip-hop choreography.

It occurred to Pippa that the demands of starring in a Miss Bill production *and* working at Cheetah had become so all-consuming that she seemed to be rotating in her own extended orbit, far from Max, Christina, Dante, and especially Vanity, who still remained missing in action.

The once-reigning queen of the fabulous five had isolated herself from everyone. For weeks after the accident, Pippa had made every overture possible—phone calls, home visits, e-mails, text messages, special care packages. But never once had Vanity responded. Finally, Pippa stopped trying. And now she found herself in a new rhythm of life, albeit one that included a constant stream of lies to keep her racy job a secret.

Of course, the *Sweet Charity* show was a glorious alibi for late-night absences. After all, *nobody* could know that she was strutting her stuff at Cheetah for fistfuls of dollars.

The default response to her mum and her friends for not being around had become the play. But she also made up a job as a part-time assistant to an entertainment promoter. That helped explain the sudden appearance of expensive new clothes and accessories.

God! Keeping all the lies and half-truths straight had become exhausting. Pippa was pulling down squillions at Cheetah, and the shoe boxes of cash tucked away in her closet were big to bursting. The truth was, she could afford a car now. A brand-new one! But she had a feeling that such a purchase would be the tipping point, the one conspicuous move that might arouse too much curiosity and expose her secret life. So she rammed around Miami in a beat-up Chevrolet, a total spazmobile that made Dante's Honda look like a luxury ride.

Poor Max. Sometimes Pippa felt downright witchy for dodging him so often, but what else could she do? Between nailing down her role in the play and working shifts at the club, there was no time. And, to be truthful, the little matter regarding his father had become more complicated. Pippa much preferred the man to the boy, so she was hardly killing herself to spend time with Junior.

Max *could* have been starring in *Sweet Charity* as Vittorio, one of her character's love interests. He won the role hands down, thanks to his electric charisma and effortless comic timing. But his smart-ass mouth and lazy work ethic did *not* go over well with Miss Bill, who promptly booted Max out of the cast and assigned him the thankless job of promoting ticket sales. Being the son of a movie star got you nowhere with Miss Bill.

"Sweat and tears, people!" Pippa could hear Miss Bill's constant refrain boomerang in her mind at random points throughout the day. "That's all I want to see. Sweat and tears. Add some blood to that and you just might have a chance in hell of doing this for a living."

The DJ cranked up hard-charging rock music, blasting Miss Bill's voice out of Pippa's head and breaking her private reverie. Every night she left Cheetah with a ringing in her ears. It was a minor miracle that she could still hear.

She exited the stage in a huff, ran straight into Vinnie, and decided to let her displeasure about tonight's cheap customers be known. "This crowd totally sucks shit!"

"What were you doing up there?" Vinnie asked.

"Something different!"

Vinnie pointed to Brandi, a new girl who had the patrons roaring like lions as Def Leppard's "Pour Some Sugar on Me" exploded from the speakers. "Stick with the tried and true, Star Baby. Singing is the last thing these guys want to see your mouth do." He cackled and pinched her ass. "Now go freshen up. There's a VIP waiting upstairs just for you." He gave her a knowing wink.

Pippa dashed into the locker room.

Hellcat was busy fastening the top of her American flag bikini. "Loved your number, honey," she said with a sneer. "But I think that act would go over better at a gay cabaret."

Pippa ignored her. Brilliantly. It was either that or stomp on the bitch. She stripped down, redressing quickly in a La Perla Marvel bra, Roberto Cavalli satin roll-up shorts, and Michael Kors suede slingbacks. Then she flashed a wet tongue over her lips to make the Galaxy Girl lipstick by Nars shine brighter.

Twirling in a tight pirouette, Pippa surveyed the goods. She looked hot. Scorching, in fact. A fiery, sun-burnished, sex bomb blonde. Oh, yes. Star Baby knew how to give off killer heat.

She could practically feel Hellcat's hateful gaze sizzling between her shoulder blades. The scabby whore was crazy mad with jealousy. Pippa was younger, hotter, Vinnie's favorite, and the Lair girl of choice for the club's most important customer—Max Biaggi.

Knowing that he was upstairs waiting for her—and her alone—filled Pippa with a heady satisfaction, and if she thought about it long enough, then she just might start gushing like a Roman fountain.

Max Biaggi did something to Pippa. Something that his son didn't do. And that was set her body on fire with lust. Just being in the same room with him sent delicious quickenings into the pit of her stomach.

Often Pippa wondered if those butterflies were feelings for him or anxiety over the dangerous game she continued to play as private dancer to the father and best mate to the son, a game that went on with both of them blissfully unaware that they shared her.

Unlike the junior version, big Max seemed to have all the time in the world when it came down to the matter of sex. He was in total control and in no rush to do anything.

Pippa found this exquisitely appealing. Here it was, a few months since their first meeting, and Pippa had barely touched him. Last time she was allowed to faintly graze his body with her breasts during a dance. Yet the whole time all she wanted to do was cling to him passionately and beg him to take her . . . any way that he chose.

"Got another private dance with Mr. Hollywood?" Hellcat asked, blocking Pippa's path as she turned to leave.

Pippa attempted to move around her.

Hellcat stopped her with a snake-bite grip to the arm, fake nails digging into the skin, nearly breaking it. "Not so fast, Star Cunt. I'm talking to you."

Pippa winced at the pain. "I would appreciate it very much if you would let go of me." Her voice remained calm, even though she wanted to scream bloody curses at the stench trench in front of her.

"Oh, how proper," Hellcat said with a snort, mocking Pippa's British accent as she let go of her arm. "You think that giving private dances to a big movie star makes you better than the rest of us?" She stepped closer, blowing her warm, stale Marlboro Lights–infused breath directly into Pippa's face. "But one day you'll find out the hard way what you really are."

Pippa matched Hellcat glare for glare. "Well, right now I'm sick to my stomach. So please excuse me." And then she stalked toward the exit.

"Keep dreaming, Star Baby," Hellcat called out. "That's right. Keep dreaming about Mr. Hollywood. Every whore has to hold on to something."

Pippa refused to look back, banishing Hellcat from her mind as she made her way up the stairs to the Lair, filled with a delectable wonder. How far would Max Biaggi take the fun tonight?

When she stepped inside, music wafted softly from the iPod stereo. The Eagles were his favorite band. Tonight's song was "Life in the Fast Lane."

Pippa smiled.

"Happy Thanksgiving, Star Baby."

Max Biaggi's voice drove her crazy. Every time he spoke, she felt a little thump in the gut.

With a quick zap of the remote control, he tuned out Don Henley. "What are you thankful for tonight?"

Pippa was suddenly struck by the strangeness of the circumstances. Max Biaggi Jr. was home alone on this holiday, drinking himself into oblivion and missing her company. Meanwhile, his father was front and center, paying top dollar for it. "I'm thankful that you came to see me."

He poured her a glass of champagne. "Good answer."

"It's the truth," Pippa said. And she meant it.

Max Biaggi patted the space next to him on the sofa. "Sit right here. I want you to rest those gorgeous feet."

Pippa settled down beside him.

Max Biaggi reached down for her left foot. His hands were warm and strong, his fingers long and masculine. Lovingly, he undid the strap on her slingback and slipped off the shoe, massaging her foot.

Pippa gasped, just a little. She watched in wide-eyed wonder as he raised her naked foot, moving it closer . . . closer . . . and closer to his mouth.

"Sing me a song, Star Baby. The men downstairs don't deserve to hear your voice. Save it just for me. In fact, save everything just for me."

Pippa nodded in complete agreement, her heartbeat thumping in her ears.

And then Max Biaggi began to suck her toes like they were the tastiest delicacy in the world.

The sensation of his worshipful lips and tongue shot like a quivering arrow into her secret place.

"Sing, Star Baby, sing."

So Pippa did the honors, serenading him with her second-favorite number from *Sweet Charity*.

"If my friends could see me now!"

It was Thanksgiving, a holiday that most families celebrated together, so Vanity's father was away, of course. Something about one of his label's top selling artists being arrested in Los Angeles on a murder charge.

Vanity didn't care. After all, what did it matter anyway? There was a difference between just showing up and being present. When Simon St. John turned in an appearance, it was always the former. He was nothing more than a body occupying space, never fully engaged, never really involved at all.

Usually, holidays were a passport to misery, a painful reminder of all the simple things that Vanity wanted but would never have—a mother who actually gave a damn, a father who could conjure up enough interest to fake it once or twice a year.

"Expect people to behave as they always have in the past," Dr. Parker had told her. "That way you won't set yourself up for disappointment."

This Thanksgiving, for the first time since she could ever remember, was free of heartache. Finally, Vanity knew how to condition herself to embrace the day with no expectations, to truly be thankful for the blessings she did have. And it was a wonderful feeling.

She was thankful for life itself. The accident almost ended hers, and so many times in the grueling months that followed the crash, she wished that it had. But not anymore. The power to start again was within her, just waiting to be tapped.

She was thankful for family. Lala, Gunnar, and Mercedes had been the ones to see her through the rain. And today the four of them were enjoying a lovely celebration all their own, indulging in a feast prepared by Lala, watching the *March of the Penguins* DVD, and walking along South Beach. Walter "Steak" Williams, Vanity's relentless physical therapist, dropped by with a delicious caramel cake that his grandmother had made. It was a perfect day.

She was thankful for friends, too. Even months after her self-imposed exile, she could feel their support, as if by some psychic connection. Dr. Parker had helped Vanity reconcile the irrational anger and work through the conflicting feelings. They were pulling for her full recovery and wanting her back to complete the social circle. She knew that now.

Sighing with a mixture of general exhaustion and shame for her caloric over-indulgence, Vanity wearily pushed her second, half-eaten slice of caramel cake away from her. "Somebody stop me. I'm an absolute pig."

Lala laughed. "That's good, yes? It means your appetite is back."

"Well, I wish it would go away and take this ass I don't recognize with it," Vanity said, slapping her butt to emphasize her displeasure with the unavoidable weight gain.

"A little junk in the trunk is a good thing," Steak said with a wink. "Now you've got a Beyonce booty."

Vanity gave him a faux glare. "Get out and take your fattening cake with you. I'm never eating again." But then her gaze fell upon the plate that was just within reach. A luscious gob of rich caramel was right there, practically begging to be devoured. "Oh, fuck it." And then Vanity shamelessly made the temptation disappear.

Lala and Steak roared with laughter as Gunnar and Mercedes sat enraptured in front of a Hi-Five video, blissfully unaware.

Vanity pointed an accusing finger at Steak. "We've got just over a month to get this excess fat off my ass, not to mention every other part of my body."

Max was hosting a New Year's Eve bash, a charity event for Hurricane Wilma victims of all things. Ha! Max Biaggi Jr. and charity—two things that definitely didn't sound right in the same sentence.

But Vanity planned to be there, to shock everybody with a surprise entrance, and by the end of December she would be ready—physically, emotionally, and spiritually. Her entire world was being turned right side up again.

"A little thickness is healthy," Steak argued. "Any man would take Jennifer Lopez over Lindsay Lohan."

Stubbornly, Vanity shook her head. "The weight's coming off before New Year's. That party's going to be my official coming out."

Steak and Lala trades amused glances.

"As a living and breathing person!" Vanity clarified with exaggerated frustration. "Although considering my history with guys, maybe I *should* become a lesbian. I mean, I couldn't do any worse." She rolled her eyes. "And on that pathetic note, how about just one more bite of cake . . ."

From: Vanity

The bitch is back. Don't believe it? Turn around and see
for yourself.

11:59 pm 12/31/05

chapter nine

the bitch *was* back. And goddamn, did she ever know how to make an entrance.

Max couldn't believe it.

Vanity St. John was waltzing into the party at one minute before midnight on the last day of the year, upstaging every drunken New Year's kiss in the process.

"Look at her!" he exclaimed to Shoshanna. "How awesome is that?"

"Near-death accidents apparently agree with her," Shoshanna said. "She looks better than ever."

Jesus, he was almost crying. Shit. He *was* crying. "You don't know how worried I've been, Sho. I'd all but given up on her."

Max's eyes were wet with tears as he ran toward Vanity,

breaking every land speed record in the books to get the first hug, embracing her with more warmth and emotion than he knew was possible for him. He released his hold to kiss her lightly on the lips, then drew back to get a serious look at her.

Oh, yes, the bitch was *definitely* back.

Every girl at the warehouse bash was trying way too hard tonight. Too much skin. Too much makeup. Too much jewelry. And in walks Vanity St. John to show them all how easy it should be.

She wore a man's Banana Republic white dress shirt unbuttoned to the navel, Imitation of Christ drainpipe jeans, and a pair of brown Burberry riding boots. Her hair, once knife-blade straight, was now a wild mane of tangled jet-black curls.

There were words for girls who looked this good. Right now Max could only think of one . . . "magnificent." He laughed to himself, thinking about the crazy gossip that had been roaming on message boards, in chat rooms, and between the covers of tabloid trash weeklies for months.

Rumor: Vanity St. John had gotten fat. Fact: The girl's ass could still scoop out a guy's guts and make him a slave for life.

Rumor: Vanity St. John was confined to a wheelchair. Fact: Not only was the girl standing on two feet, her wildside walk could still substitute for Viagra.

"God, I can't believe you're here!" Max exclaimed, hugging her once more. "But you've completely screwed up my schedule. I'd planned on getting a blow job right after the countdown."

Vanity laughed. "Well, that explains why Ryan Seacrest is outside standing next to your Porsche."

Max grabbed her hand, brushing his lips across her knuckles. "Oh, baby, you *are* back. Like Mariah. The *Glitter* days are over."

Vanity's green eyes gleamed like the emeralds they were. "Forget Mimi. It's 'the Emancipation of *Vanity.*'"

As the awareness of her presence began to ripple through the crowd, word spread fast. The Vanity St. John sighting was *not* a hoax.

Suddenly, everyone was watching her and talking about her. But Vanity ignored them with a metaphysical calm that only famous people possessed in public situations.

Max howled at the ceiling. "Let's get druuuuuunk!" Then he punched a fist to the DJ, who was surrounded by go-go dancers on the main floor platform.

The Missy Underground mix of Ashlee Simpson's "L.O.V.E." went down. Pharrell and Gwen Stefani's so-sick-it-should-be-illegal duet came up.

"So can I have it like that?" Max sang.

"You got it like that," Vanity sang right back.

The year 2006 had arrived, and if the first few minutes were any indication, then Vanity knew that it was going to be a fantastic one. The last six months had been hell on earth. But right now she felt positively bulletproof.

She took in the scene. Max's New Year's Eve Screw Wilma party was hotter than any event had a right to be. Every dollar was going to help victims recover from damages caused by Hurricane Wilma. Nobody believed Max had it in him, but the boy could give good charity when properly inspired.

Rich kids were paying a five-hundred-dollar cover to have wicked fun. Poor kids were getting a little help. And Max Biaggi Jr. was lording over it all, earning high fives from every direction. Her best friend had taken it up a notch. He was a true nightlife impresario.

They were partying in an abandoned warehouse on the outskirts of South Beach. The cavernous space had been transformed into a club paradise. Thirty thousand square feet and four stories of decadent fun from top to bottom.

Liquor was flowing like lava from a volcano. Beautiful girls danced. Cool guys dreamed up schemes to get them into bed. And the also-rans watched from the sidelines, wishing and praying that they could be a VIP thoroughbred, if only for one night.

"This is amazing," Vanity praised, taking in the glass-walled showers on the third floor, complete with hot running water and naked dancers under spray jets.

"Oh, this is nothing," Max teased. "We haven't hit the I-can't-freaking-believe-it zone yet."

"What?" Vanity demanded to know, finding the intrigue delicious.

"Well, it *is* New Year's Eve," Max pointed out. "Something awesome has to happen. I want Screw Wilma to be *the* holy shit party of the year. Watch this." He gave the DJ a signal.

"What's up, Miami?" The mix master's smooth, buttery voice boomed over the sound system. "There's a surprise guest who's here tonight to throw it down, and let me just say this . . . you're not going to forget where you were for New Year's Eve 2005, so prepare to get buck wild, and show some love for Grammy Award–winning and platinum recording artist . . . *Ashanti!*"

The crunchy guitar intro of "Only U" sent the party people into a frenzy of screams and applause as they jockeyed for position to get a closer look at the princess of hip-hop, who appeared on the main platform amidst a cloud of colored smoke, resplendent in a gold-sequined microdress and flanked by three backup dancers.

Ashanti ran through a high-energy twenty-minute set that also included "Foolish," "Rain on Me," "Rock wit U

(Awww Baby)," and "Still on It" before exiting to a thunderous ovation.

Vanity rushed over to Max, who was glowing with an impossible radiance. "How did you manage to pull off *that?*"

Max gave a no-big-deal shrug. "I know people who know people."

And then Vanity saw him. Dante Medina. He was making his way through the revelers, pointing at Max with an accusing index finger that should be the new sign language for "you sneaky son of a bitch."

From the opposite direction she saw Christina, clapping ostentatiously and shadowed by her new friend, Keiko Nakamura.

When Dante and Christina reached Vanity, genuine hugs went back and forth, the easy bells of chatter began to chime, and everybody decided that they needed another drink, preferably a jolt.

Max solicitously played barkeep and worked fast to produce five Red Bulls, then led the group up one level to a private VIP area.

"You look *unbelievable,*" Christina breathed as something close to love light shone from her eyes.

"Everybody does," Vanity demurred.

"This is Keiko," Christina said. "She's new to MACPA this semester."

"I've heard so much about you," Vanity said kindly, even though most of her information had come from Max, who absolutely hated the girl and wanted her exported back to San Francisco.

"Ditto," Keiko sneered. "You're sort of like a legend at MACPA. But I can't figure out why. Besides being a mannequin, exactly what *is* your artistic talent?"

"Keiko!" Christina admonished.

Imperviously, Vanity peered down at the short, rude girl. "The acting program is my major, and I do have the skill set. For example, right now I'm pretending to be interested in this conversation. Even when I'm so over it."

Just as Vanity walked away, a hand reached out for hers. Instantly, she recognized the touch.

"Hey, stranger," Dante said.

"Hey." She hoped the easy smile on her face told him that the past drama was officially a million years old.

"It's good to see you," he said. "Really, it is." One beat. "Especially on dry land."

Vanity parted her lips to speak.

"Ugh—bad joke," Dante said, covering his eyes with embarrassment.

"Not *so* bad," Vanity said easily. "I mean, somebody had to bring up the obvious."

"No hard feelings?"

She waved off the notion. "Bygones."

Dante smiled. "You do look beautiful tonight."

"I feel beautiful," Vanity said. "On the inside for a change. I've been doing a lot of work with my therapist. I've been meditating. I can finally exercise again. Everything is starting to come together."

"That's great. I'm happy for you."

Vanity found herself prolonging the moment, if only to gaze into Dante's dark eyes. The attraction she felt for him was still electric. His handsomeness knew no bounds. "I'm not the same girl who kicked you out of that boat. I want you to know that."

Before Dante could respond, a young girl broke between them, crushed her body against his, and kissed him deeply on the mouth. "Rule number one: On a night like this, never separate yourself from your date at midnight."

"Happy New Year, Dante," Vanity said stoically. And then she left him there to learn the rest of the rules from his new girl.

Max stood back, a smile of accomplishment and pleasure on his face. Vanity St. John's return was on everybody's lips. So was the Ashanti concert coup. Both incidents were already solidifying their place in the pantheon of Miami party folklore.

Christina glanced around curiously. "Where's Pippa?"

The question instantly tripped Max into a bittersweet

mood. "Rehearsing for the play, working her mystery job, off somewhere with Waldo, who knows?"

Pippa had promised to be here. She'd promised him a kiss at the stroke of midnight, too. But these days a promise from her didn't mean shit.

Max raised his Red Bull to no one in particular. "To bling addicts everywhere." After drinking deep, he crushed the can and cut through the packed crowd, working hard to push the disappointment out of his mind.

This was his party. This was his room. The collective energy swarmed all around him. He decided the night should end with a bang.

Max grabbed the eyes of a Latina girl wearing a silver dress that was condom tight. Madonna's "Hung Up" had her wiggling about like the slut he would need after a few more drinks.

He bellied up to the bar and challenged the guy behind it. "I need a Seven and Seven as fast as humanly possible, man."

In a nanosecond, Max was staring at the drink.

Shoshanna was slouched over at his side, blitzed but still going strong. She grabbed Max's poison and sent at least a third of it down her throat. "Happy New Year."

"How much have you had tonight?"

"I'm still standing up, so obviously not enough."

"Spoken like a true alcoholic."

"You should know."

Max half smiled, repossessed his drink, and affectionately bumped Shoshanna with his shoulder.

Their stepmonster was at home, passed out in front of a television blaring "Dick Clark's New Year's Rockin' Eve." Their father was God knows where. Maybe making another crap movie. Maybe cheating on his second wife with his likely third wife. Who knew? And who cared?

"What's Dante's story?" Shoshanna asked.

Max looked at her with suspicion. "Why?"

"I don't know." But her voice took on a dreamy quality that said she did. "He's hot."

"Don't even think about it," Max snapped.

"How come?"

"He's too young and inexperienced for you."

Shoshanna giggled, twirling the Canon PowerShot looped around her wrist. "I got my picture made with Ashanti."

"Good for you." Max grinned at her proudly. "See, that's what a fifteen-year-old girl should be excited about."

"The Miz from 'The Real World' was here about an hour ago. He signed one of my boobs."

"And the moment is ruined." Max chased down the Seven & Seven.

"Somebody took a picture of it. Here, I'll show you."

She fiddled with the digital camera, flipping over the view screen.

A few clicks later, Max saw the image. There was Mike the Miz, black Sharpie in hand, marking up his sister's exposed implant. "Nice, Sho. Remind me to add that to the family album."

Shoshanna continued going through her shots. "There's me and Ashanti. She's so pretty. And sweet, too. She gave me a bottle of her new perfume. It's called Precious Jewel."

Max hooked an arm around her. "You're a precious jewel."

Shoshanna knocked him playfully. "That sounded so retarded." She clicked onward. "Oh, look, here I am with J.J."

Max felt his body tense. He peered closer. The image had been taken tonight. His gaze swept over the warehouse with laser intensity. "Where is he?"

Shoshanna was barely paying attention. "Huh? I don't know. I saw him right before Ashanti went on. Do I look fat in this picture?"

Max left in search of J.J. A quickly lit anger bubbled to the surface. It was about to boil over. He walked fast, searched fast, thought fast.

Max noticed a striking girl with braces huddled in a corner, crying over what looked to be boyfriend troubles.

He noticed a dumb jock on the second floor, dry heaving over a garbage bin while his buddies stood around and laughed. But still no J.J.

He passed another bar, stopped for a Seven & Seven, then let it loose, practically gargling with it. A serious buzz kicked in. That's when he saw J.J. on level three, chatting up one of the shower dancers.

Max hustled up via a short cut. As he squeezed past a loudspeaker, the sound waves of Kelly Clarkson's "Since U Been Gone" hit hard, vibrating his chest wall on impact.

Finally, Max reached him.

J.J. announced himself with the unmistakable aroma of expensive pot.

"What are you doing here?" Max demanded.

"You don't return calls."

"Why should I?" His gaze fell on the megabanner declaring it 2006. "Our business was over and done with *last year.*"

"UPN dropped my option. It's not even pilot season yet. I got one stupid guest shot on 'Veronica Mars,' and it was barely a walk-on."

Max shrugged. "I think you've got me confused with someone who actually gives a shit."

J.J. gave a bored yawn. "I figured as much. That's why I sold the copy of the video I kept to an interested party. It uploaded at midnight. Go to ScrewVanity-dot-com. See for yourself."

Max felt his heart sink, and the Seven & Sevens chose this moment to seriously kick in. He moved off to the side, weaving slightly, gripping the cold steel railing for support.

Down below, Vanity was burning up the dance floor, looking happy, healthy, and totally at peace. She stole a glance upward. She saw Max. She raised a hand to wave, then caught sight of J.J. The luminous smile on her face closed. The alarm in her eyes told Max that she knew the bottom line.

He shut his eyes, hoping she could handle the nightmare that was certain to unfold. When he opened them a split second later, Vanity was gone. And the Screw Wilma crowd partied until morning light.

Happy Fucking New Year.

From: Keiko

Look out your window.

9:36 pm 1/17/06

chapter ten

It's cold," Keiko said. "Let me in!"

"But my mom's home!" Christina's voice was a hushed whisper.

"I know. I saw her car. That's why I didn't ring the doorbell. Come on, I'm freezing my ass off."

Christina worked fast to push open the window and help Keiko crawl through it. "What are you doing here? This is crazy."

Keiko grinned. "Sometimes crazy can be good."

Christina shot a fearful look to the closed bedroom door. "We have to be quiet. There's no lock."

Keiko smoothed out her punk schoolgirl skirt and began poking around Christina's things. "What's this?" She snatched some unfinished pages of *Harmony Girl* from the drafting table.

"Just a *manga* I'm working on. It's nothing, really." Christina moved to take possession of her work.

Keiko darted out of reach, still inspecting the illustrations. "Wait a minute. This is that Vanity girl."

"It's based on her, yeah," Christina said, working hard to sound casual. "I used some pictures of her as a model sheet. No big deal."

Keiko remained frustratingly out of reach. "Have you watched the Internet video of her banging that guy? It's pretty hot."

Christina shrugged. "I can't get that kind of stuff on my computer. My mom's got a filter on our DSL line."

"But you'd watch it if you could, wouldn't you?" Keiko taunted. "Dirty, dirty girl." She laughed.

"No, I wouldn't do that," Christina snapped, growing increasingly annoyed by this intrusion. "She's a friend of mine."

Keiko laughed at her. "But don't you still want to see what she looks like naked?"

Christina experienced a flush of heat rise up her neck. "What's your problem, Keiko?"

"Oh, I think it's *your* problem. You're the one in love with *Vanity.*"

"No, I'm not!" Christina's voice rose louder than she intended it to.

Keiko put a finger to her black-painted lips. *"Shhh.*

What if Mommy hears you?" And then she rolled around on the bed, tickled pink by her discovery. "Oh, Christina. You're so repressed. Baby girl, you're like a 1950s housewife. Did you ever see *Far from Heaven* with Julianne Moore? That's who you are. Only instead of the black gardener, you've got it bad for the porn queen celebutante." Keiko laughed again. "It's nothing to be ashamed about. She's gorgeous. You've got great taste in women. But Vanity's straight. So you really need to move on. Trust me. I know of what I speak. I've known a million secret lesbians who've fallen for their straight girlfriends, and it *never, ever* works out. Either way, you have to part company. If something *does* happen, it's usually a mistake in a moment of weakness—tequila is typically a culprit—and then everything gets all weird. The friendship never recovers. On the other hand, if something *doesn't* happen, then that's even worse, because the agony just drags on and on. You tell yourself that you're just friends, but deep down you know that there are much stronger feelings not being recognized. And all that does is keep you from seeking out a real relationship."

Christina felt sick to her stomach, the kind of upending, nervous anxiety brought on by unavoidable truths. "Maybe you should just go, Keiko."

"Why? I just got here." Absently, she picked up Christina's iPod and began scrolling through the playlist.

"Oh my God—Ricky Martin? Baby girl, that is so lame. You have to delete him."

Christina snatched the iPod from Keiko's hands. "Just leave! Crawl back out the window and go home!"

Keiko sighed. "Okay. But help me up first." She stretched out a hand.

Christina huffed irritably and reached for it.

That's when Keiko yanked her toward the bed, playfully wrestling Christina onto her back with her hands pinned overhead.

"Get off me," Christina demanded softly.

Keiko shook her head no, positioning herself astride Christina, knees locked against her hips. "What's the most you've ever done with a girl?"

Christina swallowed hard. "I don't know."

Keiko laughed. "You don't know? What kind of an answer is that?"

Christina was burning with physical curiosity. She felt something alive inside her. And she was almost ready to abandon all inhibitions to find out what that might be.

"Has a girl ever done this to you?" Keiko punctuated the question by moving down to press her mouth against Christina's.

As if in answer, Christina's lips fell open in wonder, inviting Keiko's tongue to twine with hers. The sensation of Keiko's piercing hardware felt strange. It was a tantalizing surprise, though, velvet warmth against velvet warmth, and then the sudden texture of cool metal.

Christina was so lost in the moment that she didn't even know her mother had stepped inside the room until Paulina spoke.

"It's late, Christina." Her voice took on a robotic quality.

Christina froze.

"Please ask your company to go home."

And then her mother left the room and quietly shut the door behind her.

Keiko giggled. "Total denial must run in the family."

Christina just lay there, immobilized, terrified of what her mother's next move might be. Because there would definitely be one. Of that she was certain.

Vanity's celebutante fame had triggered its share of disturbing attentions. She was no stranger to hostile letters, requests for money, and the occasional marriage proposal. The rumors surrounding her accident had been daunting, too. But nothing had prepared her for the aftermath of having a sex tape floating around the Internet.

The video's online presence lasted just one week. That's how long it took for her father's lawyers to build their legal salvo—a one-hundred-million-dollar lawsuit with temporary restraining orders, preliminary injunctions, and writ of seizures against Jayson James, a host of Internet service providers, and a laundry list of sites ranging from famous-teenwhores.com to Gawker.

Even though the legal offensive had been immediately effective, there were still copies of the tape to be found if someone Googled deep enough. The only silver lining was the knowledge that, no matter the outcome of the pending case, J.J. had already been buried in enough attorney fees to ruin him financially. And the scandal had effectively killed his modeling career, as well.

But nothing could kill the online haters. Message boards exploded with Vanity St. John hate talk. The compulsion to know what people were saying about her was far more powerful than her will to turn away from it, no matter how bad the postings made her feel. And so she continued to read them, sometimes over and over again.

Posted By: ScoobyD

Created In: Forum: StarGazing

Posted: Jan 17, 2006 10:33 pm

This girl is a total skank. I hope dude was wearing like a whole box of condoms and got a shot of penicillin after. lol. I'd still do her, though.

Posted By: Celia

Created In: Forum: StarGazing

Posted: Jan 17, 2006 10:31 pm

Why is this completely NON talented girl in every magazine that I pick up? If I wanted fashion tips from a total hoebag, I'd go to the Bunny Ranch, okay?

P.S. I heard Vanity's mother is a hoebag, too. I guess the apple is still ON the tree! Ha!

Posted By: BruceD

Created In: Forum: StarGazing

Posted: Jan 17, 2006 10:27 pm

Why does this chick call herself Vanity? Cuz she's a "Nasty Girl" who likes that sugar from the candy cane. Come on down to Dothan, AL, Vanity. I've got some for ya, too, baby!

Posted By: KatieGirl99

Created In: Forum: StarGazing

Posted: Jan 17, 2006 10:21 pm

Vanity has completely degraded herself with this video. Wow, she can get drunk as a skunk and be uninhibited on camera with a stoned-out cheeseball male model. She's so cool! I wish I could do that! On second thought, NOT! If Vanity didn't meet the official "beauty" standard, then nobody would care about her at all.

Posted By: SnoopCat

Created In: Forum: StarGazing

Posted: Jan 17, 2006 10:02 pm

A buddy of mine was in a gang bang with Vanity and said that the tape will be hitting the Net soon. She took on seven guys in a Miami hotel. This babe's hardcore.

Posted By: EarthAngel

Created In: Forum: StarGazing

Posted: Jan 17, 2006 9:51 pm

This bitch needs to listen to Mary J. Blige's "No More Drama"! I'm sick of her crazy shit. First she drives her car into a semi and breaks her leg in a million places. Now she's crying about some sex tape that she made her damn self. Somebody should tie a cement block to this pork slit and throw her into Biscayne Bay. She's not even that hot if you ask me. Peace out!

On nights like this, Vanity soothed herself with alcohol. And plenty of it. Drinking dulled her senses while she waited for the insult axes to fall. She knew that everybody at MACPA was reading these boards, because the worst of the lot always found their way back to her.

The sheer onslaught had bell-jarred her into an emotional wreck again. Just weeks ago she had felt so strong, so hopeful, so ready to take on the future. But tonight she felt all of that initiative slipping away again.

From: Mimi

I got a call from VH-1's SURREAL LIFE. They're interested. Thoughts?

2:11 pm 2/10/06

chapter eleven

It was opening night for *Sweet Charity* at MACPA, starring Pippa Keith in the title role. With every seat in the auditorium full and the balcony standing room only, the anticipation for the rise of the curtain sizzled with palpable electricity.

Out here, in the audience, sat Vanity St. John, Lala on one side, Max on the other. She fidgeted in her seat, throwing glances around. A few rows up, she watched Christina and Keiko slip into their seats and giggle like two schoolgirls who'd just left the water running in the bathroom.

Lala patted Vanity's hand with sweet support. "This will be fun, yes?"

Vanity returned a noncommittal nod. The truth was, right now she'd give up her firstborn child for a shot of vodka. Something told her that she was going to need it.

Max leaned in to whisper, "Five words—spring break in New York."

Vanity shot him a curious look.

"We have access to beaches all year long. Let's do the city thing. I'll make all the arrangements. I'm thinking about hosting a rooftop party in midtown, too. We've done Miami to death. Let's take Manhattan."

Vanity vaguely agreed. As long as liquor was in ample supply, she really didn't care where they went or who was there.

Dante arrived late and settled into his seat next to Max, acknowledging Vanity and Lala with a smile and a half wave.

"You're late, bitch," Max teased him. "I assume you were backstage volunteering as a fluffer for the chorus boys."

"How did you know?" Dante joked.

Max touched his chin. "You've got some come right here under your lip."

Dante laughed.

Vanity smiled wanly. She continued to be frustrated by Dante's indifference and couldn't shake the idea that they were destined to be more than a doomed summer fling. But he made no attempts to reconnect. Now they just seemed to merely tolerate each other.

The house lights went down.

As the darkness swamped over her, Vanity experienced a tight feeling in her chest and took in a sharp breath, steeling herself to remain calm. Sometimes it required superhuman effort to talk herself out of a total meltdown for no reason at all. But emotional toughness was Vanity's home turf.

She survived childhood. She fought through the car accident. She was enduring the Internet scandal. And she would get over Dante, too.

The play commenced, and Vanity became instantly overwhelmed by Pippa's uninhibited energy and raw stage finesse. She sang and danced with such determination and gusto that Vanity forgot she was watching a friend in a school production.

All around her the audience hummed with excitement.

After one of the bigger numbers, more than one person erupted with, "Who *is* that girl?"

Somewhere in the subterranean recesses of Vanity's mind, she felt a bitter resentment toward Pippa. The girl was both talented *and* gorgeous. When people talked about her later tonight, it wouldn't be because she wore a new Dolce & Gabbana dress, had closed her eyes and crashed into a truck, or got drunk and had no idea a guy was filming her during sex. It would be because she brought down the house with authentic Broadway dazzle.

Jealousy stewed within her, a simmering cauldron of why-not-me regrets and insecurities. Casting a sideways glance to Max, Vanity noticed that his attention was gridlocked onto Pippa, his eyes completely transfixed.

That's when the evil little wish crept down the chimney of Vanity's brainstem. Secretly, she wanted Pippa to hit a sour note, to miss a dance step, or maybe to fall flat on her face, anything to break the enchanting spell that she'd cast over the crowd.

And then, all of a sudden, as if God himself had sent down a thunderbolt, it happened.

Eardrum-piercing feedback ripped through the speakers, tormenting the audience and pushing the stage players off their marks.

Pippa had been midsong, knocking them dead. Now she looked terrified and disoriented, like a wounded animal on the side of a busy road.

Miss Bill dashed over to the sound board, where two junior classmen fearfully fumbled with the controls. Desperately, he tried to intercede, but the theatrical dictator failed at the task.

Dante vaulted from his seat and raced over to offer assistance. In record time, he tamed the forty-channel beast with its blinking lights, pushing slides, and reading dials.

Within moments, technical order was restored.

Miss Bill openly swooned over Dante.

Pippa received a cue from the stage manager, then launched back into her performance with seamless aplomb, as if nothing had ever happened.

And Vanity sat there, steaming in the dark, working hard to tame the green-eyed monster of jealousy, as one bitter question rampaged inside her mind.

When would Dante Medina be her goddamn hero for a change?

"Just listen one more time," Dante insisted, beginning to lose patience with Juan Barba, who seemed more interested in checking out Max's little sister than anything else.

Shoshanna queued the iPod stereo to blast "Le Jazz Hot," the jaunty roof-raiser performed by Julie Andrews in *Victor/Victoria*.

Once again, Juan shook his head. "I don't hear it, man. Sounds like some gay shit to me."

Shoshanna giggled.

Juan gave her a flirtatious wink.

Dante held firm. "Nobody's tapped this track, man. I'm telling you. It could be a serious groove. Add a sick beat. Rewrite the lyric vibe to 'Le Hip-Hop.' Find a sweet honey with a killer range to sing the answer vocal. That shit would be off the hook."

But Juan didn't budge. "Man, that fancy arts school is

making you soft. I think you need to drop out and get hard."

Dante chose not to respond. He just allowed the track to play out in its entirety as he listened with quiet intensity.

The idea had come to him while watching Pippa perform her encore in *Sweet Charity*. Hip-hop artists had been cleverly mining the vaults for years to find sample tracks that could facilitate a unique sound. But so far, legendary composer/arranger Henry Mancini's "Le Jazz Hot" had yet to be plucked. Pippa's brutal rump-shaking routine to Missy Elliott's version of "Big Spender" had pulled the trigger on Dante's inspiration.

He would always remember the first time that he heard "Le Jazz Hot." Dante was seven years old and living in a dilapidated house off Eighth Street in Little Havana. Each day after school, Richard Santiago, the drag queen next door, would see after Dante until his mother arrived home.

Dressed up in full drag as Rita-Rita, a Paris dance hall diva, Richard refused Dante's pleas to watch *Spider-Man* and forced him to be an audience of one for lip-synch routines to "Le Jazz Hot," which he performed as his talent showcase in local gay bar beauty pageants. Dante heard the song at least a few hundred times that year, and the indelible melody and red-hot percussive beats had stuck with him ever since.

Deep down, he knew that his song idea was destined for hit-record status. Juan Barba was so wrong that there should be a new word for wrong. Dante's final product would be on the cutting edge and a million miles from "gay." But they would want to groove to it, too. All he needed was someone with connections to believe the same thing.

Juan stood up. "I better roll before you bust out with a cut from *The Sound of Music.*"

Dante chuckled.

Juan could still be funny, even when being a short-sighted asshole. He whispered something in Shoshanna's ear that made her giggle, then took her hand and started out. "Later, man."

"Hold up," Dante protested, reaching for Shoshanna's free hand and pulling fast. "You may take my pride out the door, but I don't think you'll be taking Max's sister."

Shoshanna swayed back and forth between Juan and Dante, laughing with delight, clearly enjoying the tug-of-war attention.

"She's fifteen," Dante said.

Juan grinned. "You shouldn't have told me that, man. Now I'm *definitely* taking her."

Max had left earlier to get a haircut and do some shopping, so it was just the three of them in the basement of the Biaggi mansion on Star Island.

"Come on, man. Stop being a punk. Let me tap this real quick. I'll bring it back just like I found it. Promise." Juan smiled. And it was the reassuring smile of a pedophile with a cute puppy and a box of candy.

Shoshanna continued to playfully swing between them.

Dante looked at her sharply. "Knock it off, Sho. This isn't funny. You're not going anywhere with this guy."

Shoshanna huffed a little, then attempted to pull free from Juan.

The Latin hip-hop/reggaetón star refused to release her. "What's up with the cock block, man? Are you pissed off that I didn't dig that song, or are you looking to hit this, too?" His eyes narrowed into slits. "No problem. We can share. Which end do you want?"

Shoshanna attempted to shake her arm free. "You're gross. Sounds like what you're looking for is a farm animal."

Juan gripped Shoshanna even tighter. "Whoa, I got a live one here!"

Shoshanna gazed fearfully at Dante, silently pleading with him to get her out of the situation.

"This isn't cool," Dante said. He wondered what stimulants Juan might be on, beyond the four cans of SoBe Adrenaline Rush from the last hour, which could easily put him at risk for caffeine psychosis.

Shoshanna managed to move closer to Dante, her bare

leg suddenly hot against his denim thigh. With the compulsiveness of a little girl picking at a scab, she pulled at her NO MEANS YES baby tee, which rose up to expose her taut belly and dove down to reveal her happy birthday breasts.

Girls like Shoshanna walked a dangerous tightrope. They grew up in a culture that cranked the illusion that stripper hotness was the number one virtue, and they lived in a world where the Juan Barba types believed that meant consent to just about anything.

"Take off," Dante said. His voice rang with the implicit threat that whatever Juan Barba started, Dante Medina planned to finish.

Juan stood there in his lightweight Sean Jean warm-up and chunky gold chains, nostrils flaring. Finally, he let go of Shoshanna with a rough shove. "The skank's all yours." And then he walked out.

The moment the door closed, Shoshanna wrapped her arms around Dante and hugged tightly. "You're the only guy besides my brother who's ever stood up for me." She laid her lips on his, pressing her nubile body against him.

Uncomfortably, Dante tried to untangle from her. "Easy, Lolita." He massaged the small of her back and gave her a platonic peck on the forehead. "By the way, if you kiss Max that way as a thank-you, then we need to see about getting the two of you booked on *Maury.*"

Shoshanna laughed, pulling a face. *"Ew.* That is *so* gross."

Dante felt a surge of avuncular, fiercely protective affection. He wondered if this is what it might feel like to have a baby sister. "I've got a craving for ice cream."

"Me, too!" Shoshanna chirped.

"Cool. Go put on some clothes that actually have fabric. I'm taking you to Marble Slab."

A month later, Simon St. John's Alacatraz Records dropped a hot track on the underground that ignited immediate airplay and mix-tape fire for Speed Freak, a new Latin rapper on the scene.

The song was called "Le Hip-Hop." It directly sampled "Le Jazz Hot." Speed Freak was the stage name for Tito Barba, Juan's youngest brother. A remix of the single got a rush release and moved over fifty thousand units in the first week.

Hearing "Le Hip-Hop" on the radio or in a club was the pain equivalent to a savage kick in the balls. It hurt that much. Dante was staring at his own dream through a looking glass.

He wanted Simon St. John to get rectal cancer and die. He wanted Juan Barba to get tea-bagged by a gang of sweaty dock workers. And he wanted Speed Freak to ship out for Iraq on land mine detail.

But Dante wasn't bitter. No, he wasn't bitter at all.

From: Keiko

I did it for a cause. Live your truth!

1:33 am 3/20/06

chapter twelve

Paulina Perez was in campaign mode. She sat in the living room, perched on the edge of the sofa, dressed up in full politically conservative armor—the navy business suit, the high-buttoned blouse, the low-heeled black pumps, and the single strand of cultured pearls.

Splayed out in front of her on the coffee table were informational materials for Salvation Pointe, a program located in Madison, Mississippi that claimed to help teenagers find true freedom from homosexuality through the power of Jesus Christ.

"I'm *not* going," Christina said defiantly. "You can't make me."

"Christina," Paulina hissed through tightly clenched

teeth. "Do you have any idea how this . . ." She stopped to clear her throat. "*Information* . . . has impacted my campaign?" Paulina stared at her archly. "Have you given any thought to that at all? I'm completely off message, and every media outlet in the country is expecting an official response to this . . . *nonsense.*"

Christina was still in shock. But she knew exactly what was happening, too. "I'm a lesbian, mom." She announced this in her best I'm-trying-to-say-this-as-simply-as-I-can tone. "That's not *information*. It's not *nonsense,* either. It's who I am."

Paulina's next words died in her throat, as if Christina's last statement had impaled her. After a long flustered moment, she found her voice again. "You're confused. And you're too young to know who you are anyway. That's why this place will be good for you."

Christina glanced down at the colorful, glossy brochure. Salvation Pointe resembled an upscale summer camp with its acres of pine trees, gleaming fresh-water lake, and spa-level accommodations. Of course, the rundown of rules indicated another experience entirely. In fact, it sounded like a prison.

No closed doors (with the exception of fifteen minutes each day for showering).

No contact with friends or family.

No outside news sources.

No music (unless preapproved Christian CDs or MP3-loaded players provided by Salvation Pointe staff).

No television.

No Internet use.

No diary or journal writing.

No mannish/boyish attire for girls.

No jewelry for boys.

Paulina expelled a long, frustrated sigh. "I knew this Keiko person would be trouble for you. Even when we were first introduced, I had a terrible feeling about that girl."

Keiko Nakamura wasn't a seventeen-year-old transfer student from San Francisco. She was a twenty-seven-year-old paid political operative for QUAN! (Queers Unite for Action Now!), a well-financed extreme advocacy group actively involved in the fight against Paulina's campaign, especially its agenda to shut down school-sponsored gay/straight alliance clubs.

It made for twisted irony—and headline news—when QUAN! published an exposé in their free alternative newspaper under the banner headline: ANTI-GAY SENATE HOPEFUL MARCHES AGAINST TEENAGE LESBIAN DAUGHTER.

After that kind of public humiliation, it seemed impossible that Christina could be sitting here and actually struggling to conjure up the hatred that Keiko Nakamura so richly deserved.

Yes, Keiko had sought out Christina's friendship based on a calculated deception. And yes, Keiko had violated Christina's confidence and taken advantage of her trusting nature for the sole purpose of using both as instruments in a political revenge that had nothing to do with Christina.

Still, she harbored little resentment toward Keiko, no matter how hard she tried. It was a dirty trick ambush to be sure, but the end result was strangely . . . *liberating*. An enormous emotional weight had been lifted.

Christina was gay. Now everybody knew it. And what was the silliest part of all? Nobody—except her own mother, of course—seemed to give a damn.

Politically, the fallout was shaping up to be severe for Paulina Perez. But personally, Christina had found the thunderbolt revelation to be . . . well, anticlimactic.

As she predicted long ago, Max's only reaction was a request to watch her make out with another girl, though he'd issued the stern stipulation that it *not* be Keiko.

Pippa had declared the news as good to glorious, telling Christina that she was much better off not having to live a life sorting out boys and their dicks. Dante had offered nothing more than a nonplussed utterance of "cool."

The most painful embarrassment concerned Vanity. In perhaps Keiko's ugliest act of all, she'd stolen finished pages of *Harmony Girl*, Christina's *shojo manga* in progress, and reprinted them in the newspaper as proof that art was indeed imitating life.

The title character was a beautiful and mysterious heroine who exquisitely resembled Vanity in face, shape, and form. Harmony Girl lived in an enchanted forest filled with magical animals, and she communicated with them only through music.

The main plot focused on a romantic triangle involving Harmony Girl's love for a dashing prince and her growing feelings for a young female artist named Lychee, who made secret trips from her village to the forest in order to obsessively sketch Harmony Girl's portrait.

There was no need to look deep. The subtextual connections could be seen on the surface. Harmony Girl was so obviously Vanity and Lychee so obviously Christina.

That her most private work had been robbed from her bedroom and splashed across the pages of a cheap newspaper was the ultimate violation. Initially, Christina feared that the homoerotic elements of *Harmony Girl* might engender fierce ridicule.

But precisely the opposite had occurred. Praise for Christina's first earnest attempt at *manga* came fast and furious. People loved the illustrations and the story. In fact, they wanted more. She was producing new pages as fast as possible and selling color copies of them directly out of her backpack! The whole experience had boosted her confidence, finally giving her the courage to apply for acceptance at the Savannah College of Art and Design.

I gave in on the argument to send you to MACPA, but I'm not wasting your college savings on art school. You're going to get a real education.

Paulina made this pronouncement often, but Christina now stood ready to defy her, no matter the consequences. If her mother made good on the threat and refused to pay for an art school, then Christina planned to secure student loans or accept Max's offer to lend her the money for tuition.

It was a wonderful feeling to finally be living honest and free. She didn't have to dread her sexuality as a dangerous subject anymore. She didn't have to stifle her most passionate interests, either.

Much of the credit should go to Keiko, too. Fraud or no fraud, she'd been the catalyst for Christina's rebirth. And now Christina found herself missing the friendship. Once the QUAN! newspaper had rolled off the printing press, Keiko dropped out of sight, never to be heard from again, save for a single late-night text message that reeked of almost apology.

The estrangement filled Christina with a deep loneliness. She refused to believe that her entire relationship with Keiko could've been a lie. They'd been too close for too long. And she especially missed Keiko's wise counsel now, during this high noon moment with Paulina regarding Salvation Pointe. Oh, yes. Keiko would *definitely* know how to handle the situation.

"This is a difficult program to get in," Paulina said, tapping the application packet with her index finger for emphasis. "The waiting list is extensive, but I've been working the phones and calling in a few political favors. The director has made a slot available for you in the residential camp."

"You're not listening!" Christina shouted. "I'm not going to that awful place!"

"Unfortunately, the timing isn't ideal," Paulina continued robotically, ignoring Christina's loud protest. "The next session begins after your spring break. Of course, this means that you'll be missing two weeks of school, but you're a smart girl. You can catch up."

"God, Mom, how can you believe this bullshit?" Christina roared. "There is no *cure* for homosexuality! This is a scam! It's nothing more than a group of manipulative bigots pimping religion to make money off horrible parents like you!" Her words were spitballs of long-suppressed rage.

Paulina's face was working hard to contain the hurt and disbelief. "A horrible parent would let you go on believing that you're a lesbian. But I plan to do everything within my power to help you live your life as you know the Lord intended. This is a phase. We wouldn't even be having this conversation if that horrible Keiko person hadn't come into our lives."

"I was a lesbian before I met Keiko," Christina said wearily. "I was born one. I've known since I was a little girl. And it's nothing that you did or didn't do that made me this way. It's just how I am. It's who I am. So deal with it. And while you're at it, get over it, too."

"You don't have a choice in this—"

"You're right," Christina cut in. "I don't have a choice about whether or not to be gay. It's not a mental disorder. There's no little white pill that's going to make me like boys. I like girls, Mom. Can you understand that? You should. You saw me in the bedroom with Keiko. I like the way girls look. I like the way they smell. I like the way they fe—"

"Stop it!" Paulina shrieked. "This is why the people at Salvation Pointe can help you. They'll teach you about morality."

Christina's mind was on fire, the flood of adrenaline raging inside her. "What's *moral* about making me feel ashamed of who I am? That's a sadistic way to raise a child. Most people would consider that abuse. So if the morality teachings are so great at this place, then maybe *you* need to go there!"

"It's abusive to want my daughter to be normal?" Paulina's tone was incredulous.

"Well, if you want me to be so normal, then why are you carrying on like I'm a freak?"

Paulina gave her a long, hard stare. "Do you want to have children one day, Christina?"

The question tripped her into a brief silence. "I don't know. I haven't really thought about it."

"Maybe you should."

"Why? I don't have to be married to a man to get pregnant or adopt a child."

"That's a selfish way to think," Paulina snapped. "In today's society, a child's best chance at success and survival is within the traditional family unit."

"Oh, please!" Christina spat. "Save the bumper sticker talk for your Rotary Club speech."

"I've had quite enough of this," Paulina announced. She stood up and smoothed out her skirt. "You're still seventeen, Christina. I decide what's best for you. Period. End of story. If necessary, the staff of Salvation Pointe will come to this house and take you by force. And it's not kidnapping when your mother signs the consent form." Her eyes gleamed as she painted the dark threat.

Christina could feel the water welling up in her eyes.

"I had every intention of canceling your spring break trip. But I've changed my mind. If only to prove to you that I'm not some kind of monster. So go to New York.

Have fun with your friends. Because when you get back, you're going to Salvation Pointe."

Christina cried a torrent of frustrated tears. "It's not going to work! I'm still going to be gay!"

Paulina's face twisted into a mask of bitterness that Christina had never witnessed before. "I would rather you commit suicide than live that life."

From: Mum

Have a GREAT spring break. Be safe and be careful in NY! Love you.

12:03 pm 4/07/06

chapter thirteen

Y ou're going to regret this," Max said.
"It's the spring break of your senior year! How many times
does that happen?"

"For some smacktards, I'm sure it comes around at least
twice," Pippa said, smiling as she took another bite of her
delicious Mediterranean salad.

"*Come on!*" Max whined, sounding like a little boy who
was being denied a new PSP game. "I need you there to
bring life to the party. Do you realize what I'm dealing with?
I've got Vanity and Christina, who could start their own
public humiliation support group. And I've got Dante, who
goes into a manic depression whenever he hears that song by
Speed Freak. The upside to my spring break is the fact that
my little sister is tagging along. How pathetic is *that*?"

"Quite," Pippa agreed. In a perverse way, she was sort of enjoying Max's minor-league miseries. Why? Because he usually gave off cockiness in radioactive waves, putting forth the invincible attitude of a seventeen-year-old guy who *always* comes out on top.

Max rolled his eyes and stabbed an artichoke heart. "Life sucks."

Only Max Biaggi Jr. could make such a doomsday pronouncement while sitting in a paradise like the Setai, an Asian-inspired luxury hotel on the edge of the Atlantic. It was landscaped with breathtaking tropical gardens and three sparkling pools. The common traveler need not inquire. Room rates started at nine hundred dollars a night. And that was for a small suite with views of a city block.

Pippa and Max were lunching in the courtyard. Surrounded by an oasis of trickling ponds and lush pergolas, they sat in sunken pods while hotel staff fussed over them like foreign royals. So if life sucked for Max right now, then the son of a bitch would *never* be satisfied.

"And then you die," Pippa said.

Max gave her a strange look.

"Isn't that the expression? 'Life sucks, and then you die.'"

"Yeah, that sounds about right," Max grumbled. "I still don't understand why you can't go. This could be one of our last big chances to party. Who knows where we'll be next year?"

Pippa sighed. "I have to work," she told him for the millionth time.

Max popped a black olive into his mouth. "I'll hire you. I'll *pay* you to come with. In fact, I'll double whatever you'd be making here."

Pippa laughed at him. Not long ago, she would've gladly accepted his offer. But now she was making her own money. She didn't need to mooch off her friends anymore. Financial independence. It was a fantastic feeling. "No, Max. I have responsibilities. I can't just take off."

He gave her a long, suspicious stare. "Are you seeing someone?"

"No," Pippa answered. "Why do you ask that?"

"Because. You *work* all the time." He gestured to the pewter kid leather Ferragamo handbag hanging on her chair. He pointed at the Swarovski crystal-covered Valentino iPod case sitting on the table. "And you're always sporting new bling." He paused a beat. "I figure you're letting some rich guy knock it out."

Pippa glared at him. "That would make me a prostitute."

Max shrugged. "Well, those shoes aren't from Payless. Obviously, you're good at your job."

"Screw you, Max! Just because I won't give *you* an all-access pass doesn't make me a hooker!" She pushed back her chair and stood up to leave.

"Sit down, drama queen. I didn't mean that like it sounded. Where I come from, sex for gifts is called a relationship."

Pippa remained standing and rummaged through her purse to find the cash to cover the entire bill. She tossed the money onto the table. *"There.* I bought *your* lunch."

"Awesome," Max remarked with a sunny indifference. "I guess this means you expect to have your way with me. We should probably get a room." He checked his watch. "I've got an hour before I have to be someplace."

Pippa wanted to slap the smug bastard across the face, so she found it infuriating when she actually started to smile. "God, you're such a snot rag!"

Max laughed. "I know. But you love me anyway. It's called charm. And having a huge inner cock doesn't hurt, either. Gives me a certain confidence that people respond to."

Pippa tilted her head to one side. "Oh, really? It makes me want to spew my guts up."

Max leaned in, close enough to inhale Pippa's breath. "Deep down, that's a sign of how much you want me to do you."

In answer, Pippa reached into her bag, pulled out a tin of Altoids, and pushed it into Max's hand. "That would sound so much better if you had one of these first."

He gave her a faux frown. "Now that's just plain mean. You know, you've been on an ego trip ever since the curtain went up on *Sweet Charity*. You were good, baby, but the show is over. I'm the original star brat, okay?"

Pippa's Nokia 7280 jingled. She checked the caller ID and started to walk away. "I have to take this, Max. It's my boss. Have a *great* trip. Call me when you get there." She waited until reaching one of the pool decks before answering. "Hi, Vinnie."

"How's my golden pussy?"

Pippa cracked a smile. Yes, Vinnie Rossetti could be disgusting, but there was something endearing about him, too. Especially the way he looked out for her well-being. "What's the big news?"

"You've got a private date tomorrow night. Notice I said 'date.' This is more than a dance, Star Baby."

Pippa could feel the butterflies take flight in her stomach. Hope swelled her heart. He'd told her to be ready on his command. It was the reason she bailed on the New York trip. "With Max Biaggi?"

"No other customer is good enough for you. His limo's picking you up at the club. Nine sharp. Dress to kill." And then Vinnie hung up.

At the sound of the click, hormones flowed that Pippa never knew existed. It was happening. The feelings were reciprocal. She loved him. He loved her. The private dances had been getting longer, the intimate conversations more meaningful. And now . . . an actual date. She was just hours away from seeing him. But already it felt like the longest wait of her life.

Pippa was red carpet gorgeous. She looked that way. She felt that way.

The Gucci wrap dress in emerald green clung to her body. But the impact was alluring, not sluttish. She loved the nostalgic 1940s silhouette with its shorter hemline, puffy cap sleeves, and subtle display of cleavage.

Her long blonde tresses were pulled back in the manner of a junior socialite and delicately held in place by a beautiful Louis Vuitton hair clip of raffia, silk, enameled metal, and pearled glass.

Pippa proudly carried her latest handbag acquisition—an amazing green crocodile purse with bamboo handles, also by Gucci. Add the chunky H. Stern chandelier earrings, the eighteen-carat-emerald Bulgari necklace, and the Ebel tank watch with diamond bezel, and only one word could accurately describe the sum of all these spectacular parts—"perfection."

Max Biaggi's limousine was scheduled to be outside the club at any moment. The truth was, Pippa could've easily waited in the parking lot. Of course, dashing into Cheetah on a faux mission to claim her Dior Addict Ultra-Gloss meant that she would be seen, fawned over, and envied. Shallow, yes. But also loads of fun.

"No you didn't, girl!" LaTonya raved as soon as she managed an unobstructed view. "No you *didn't*. Can't none of these hos around here scrub up like you. That's why they call you Star Baby. The punishment fits the crime, honey. You are flawless. Do you hear me? *Flawless.*"

LaTonya tossed a look behind her and pulled at a pigtail done up for a new dancer's Little Dutch Girl striptease. "Lexus, put that mascara down and come see this bitch."

Visibly annoyed, Lexus checked the status of her hair as she stood up. But the moment she saw Pippa, her mouth fell open in a slackened state of awe. "Holy shit! You look like a movie star," Lexus marveled.

Pippa managed a coy smile. "Oh, it's just something I put together at the last minute for my date with Max Biaggi."

"Bitch, please!" LaTonya shouted. "If this is last minute, then I'll fall out on the floor when you *really* get serious."

Pippa started to laugh, then lost all sense of humor when she saw Hellcat stalk through the locker room door, damp with sweat and streaked with bleeding Mystic Tan.

She gave Pippa an up-and-down glance, then mocked her with a raspy laugh. "Where are you off to, princess? Is it prom night?"

"This ain't no prom, child," LaTonya interceded

proudly. "Star Baby's got a romantic date with Max Biaggi!"

Hellcat put a hand to her ample hip and glowered at Pippa. "I think you've seen *Pretty Woman* one too many times. This is the real world. Strippers don't get to play Cinderella."

Pippa cast a downward glance to her Manolo Blahnik black crepe ankle-strap sandals, which dazzled with rhinestone-circle detail. "But if I do," she began silkily, "then I guess that would make you my wicked . . . step*mother*. Wouldn't it?"

Hellcat's eyes narrowed. The dig on her age had scored a direct hit, and her face was registering the psychic damage in Revlon Technicolor.

Pippa flounced toward the exit, feeling like the luckiest girl in the world.

"Hey, Star Cunt," Hellcat called out. "Don't be surprised if he only gives it to you in the ass."

Pippa stopped and spun around.

The gleam in Hellcat's eyes was bitter triumph. "He says that saves him from she's-having-my-baby scams. Trust me. I've been where you're going tonight."

Pippa refused to believe these disgusting lies. What a shagbag. "Nice try. But I think you've got Max Biaggi confused with your father, your brother, and your Uncle Charlie." Then she slipped out the exit door.

A white stretch limousine idled in the parking lot. Standing beside it was a black-suited driver. He tipped his hat to Pippa and opened the rear door with gallant flair, uttering a dutiful "Madam."

She nodded demurely and slipped inside the expansive cabin, thrilled to find Max Biaggi waiting for her, a crystal flute of Dom Pérignon at the ready. Her gaze was transfixed by the color of the bubbly, which struck her as odd.

"I added a splash of peach nectar," he explained. "It adds a certain zing."

Pippa clinked her glass to his and sipped greedily.

Max Biaggi smiled. "You like?"

Pippa nodded. "Very much."

He reached for her foot, methodically removed her shoe, and began to massage her arch with his strong, talented hands. "I've missed my babies," he whispered. "My beautiful, beautiful babies."

Pippa giggled. "Where are we going tonight? Or do you just plan to ride around town obsessing over my feet?"

"I've chartered a private plane," Max Biaggi announced. "We're taking a little trip."

Pippa was stunned. "Where?"

"That's a surprise."

Her heart picked up speed. "When are we coming back?"

"Soon." He leaned forward to run his tongue over her big toe. "Or maybe not so soon. It depends."

Pippa felt the flush of an instant anxiety. Never had she expected this. But maybe it was serendipitous. What better time to be whisked away on a secret retreat with Max Biaggi than when her mum thought she was on a senior trip to New York. "I should call—"

"Don't worry about Vinnie," he assured her, licking the space between her toes.

Pippa sank deeper and deeper into the plush leather, enjoying Max Biaggi's dedicated ministrations. This was beyond her wildest dreams—movie star, limousine, champagne, private plane. An embarrassment of riches to be sure. But thank God for that. Because when the son discovered the sins of his father and best friend, there would definitely be hell to pay. The night *needed* to be this good to fight the conflict raging inside her.

For now, though, Pippa gave in to the pleasure principle. Taking all of him in with a long, lingering gaze, Pippa decided that she loved the way he dressed. Max Biaggi was nobody's fashion victim, and he didn't try to beat the clock by throwing on clothes that belonged on someone younger. His style was masculine and timeless—a navy sportcoat, crisp white Oxford shirt, lived-in jeans, and fine Italian brown boots. There was no better outfit on a man.

Pippa factored out her fantasy from A to Z. He'd divorce Faith, his perpetually sauced wife. She didn't truly appreciate the privilege of being Mrs. Max Biaggi. Not like Pippa could. He'd propose and slide an enormous pink diamond onto her finger. The ceremony would be huge. *People* would pay megabucks for exclusive photo rights and splash them across the cover: MAX BIAGGI: SUPERSTAR ACTION HERO TAKES A HARD FALL FOR A NEW BRIDE.

The vivid image made Pippa giddy with delight. She laughed and drank more Dom Pérignon as her future husband reached for her other foot and began to lavish equally slavish attention upon it.

Suddenly, a thought struck her. This path would lead her to become Max's new stepmonster. How bizarre. She didn't understand why her friend hated his father so much. Max Biaggi was an amazing man—handsome, kind, generous, successful, and dead sexy. Granted, he probably wouldn't make the cut for dedicated daddy of the year. But Max could have it far worse. Take Pippa's father, for instance. Better yet, don't. The man was a worthless shit stabber.

As usual, Max had no idea how fortunate he was. What a spoiled brat! Maybe stepping out of his self-absorbed world for one second would help him realize the kind of pressure his father had to endure. To stay on top in Hollywood was a Mount Everest climb every day, even for a man like Max Biaggi. He kept himself in phenomenal physical shape, and his movies still killed at the box office.

But he was also a forty-four-year-old actor in an industry that worshiped the young. In fact, younger stars like Paul Walker were getting first looks at the better action scripts.

So maybe Max should try to see things from his father's perspective. Instead of whining about not having a better dad, he should try being a better son. Yes! And when the opportunity presented itself, Pippa intended to tell Max exactly that. Because the too-cool party boy *needed* to hear it. And after the advice sunk in, Max would hopefully pass the wisdom along to his trampy sister, too.

"You look beautiful tonight," Max Biaggi said. He held both of her legs, his hands cradling her calves as he gently placed her feet against his crotch. "Do you feel that?"

Pippa pressed her toes into his impressive arousal.

Max Biaggi let out a delicious groan. "That's what you do to me, Star Baby." He drank deep, refilled their glasses, and lovingly returned the Manolos back to her feet. "Are other parts of your body getting jealous?"

Pippa gave him a quizzical look, grinning.

"I spend so much time admiring your feet," he explained.

She giggled, crossing her legs just slow enough to offer him a quick flash.

He took the bait.

Pippa gave him a seductive wink. "I figure it's only a

matter of time before you learn how good the rest of me is."

Max Biaggi smiled. "Oh, I intend to, Star Baby. Believe that."

She stared at him, blissfully happy. Where they were flying remained a mystery. But Pippa didn't care because she knew one thing. And it was the only thing she needed to know.

With Max Biaggi by her side, this plane could only take her all the way to heaven.

From: Mom

Call me.

10:43 pm 4/08/06

chapter fourteen

"If I can make it there . . . I'll make it anywhere," Max sang, belting the words out in his best Sinatra voice. And he truly felt like the ultracool Rat Pack leader as he held court on the roof of this nine-story building above West 27th Street in Manhattan.

Dante laughed at him.

"Just call me the chairman of the board," Max remarked boastfully. "And based on your darker complexion and sidekick status, I guess that makes you my Sammy Davis Jr. I'll send out for an eye patch." One beat. "By the way, can you tap dance?"

Dante shook his head, grinning. "You're such a twat, man. Why am I even friends with you?"

"Because your other buddies are either in jail or delivering diapers to their baby mamas."

"These are my options?" Dante asked rhetorically. "Criminals and teenage fathers or a culturally insensitive twat who sings cheesy Sinatra tunes?"

Max reached for Dante's hand and pumped a firm, fast shake while rattling off a word string at hyperspeed. "MaxBiaggiJrgladtomeetyahowthehellareya?" Then he laughed hard at his own joke. "Shit, I'm so damn funny. I crack myself up."

Max felt like a king. After all, tonight he was reigning over Tar Beach, his first open-air party that didn't involve a pool, his first New York party ever, and judging from the beautiful people already here, the beautiful people on their way up, and the beautiful people queued up along the street, this was *his* monarchy to rule.

"And speaking of twats," he announced, gesturing to a sexy blonde gracefully navigating the freshly laid gravel in nosebleed heels. "I've got dibs on that one. But if she's rolling with a fat friend who needs a mercy screw, I'll send you a text."

"Thanks, dude. Appreciate the thought."

"Don't mention it. I'll do anything to keep you away from my sister."

"I'm never going to live that down, am I?" Dante asked wearily.

"Never," Max replied. "You saved her from that Taco Bell rapper, and now she wants to marry you."

As if by divine stage direction, Shoshanna chose this moment to dance into their line of sight, writhing seductively to a smoking remix of Chris Brown and Juelz Santana's "Run It."

Suddenly, Max's bright mood darkened. "Why is she hanging out with that son of a bitch?"

"You mean him?" Dante asked, pointing to Shoshanna's dance partner, a short, smug-looking guy outfitted in the suburban thug drag of distressed hoodie, baggie jeans, and pristine white sneakers.

Max stared daggers at him. "Yeah. He's a douche bag."

"You've said the same thing about me."

"Put it this way: I'd rather you get Sho pregnant tonight than see her hang out with that little shit for five minutes."

"Well, I have principles," Dante said. "I can't bring a child into this world knowing that you'll be the favorite uncle."

Humorlessly, Max flipped Dante the bird and bounced toward Shoshanna, tight-lipped and determined to set the girl straight.

Vlad Singer was the youngest son of a powerful Hollywood agent. He was also the baby genius type, finishing up his second year at MIT while most guys were still cramming for the SATs. But his true claim to fame was an advanced talent for recreational science.

Vlad manufactured and pushed his own club drug creations, his latest lab experiment being a lavender tablet known interchangeably as Delirium, Purple D, or System D, depending on the area of the country in which one acquired it.

Users waxed rhapsodic about Delirium, raving that its benefits were so euphorically intense that an Ecstasy trip felt like a sugar rush by comparison. And tales of sex on Purple D were already becoming the stuff of legend. Fans of System D promised orgasms that stretched on to infinity.

Tell that to the girl who died last week after taking the drug for the first time at a Dartmouth College sorority house. Is the bitch still coming? No. She's pushing up daisies in a family plot.

Max moved through the crowd, burning with protective fury. "Sho!" he shouted, grabbing her arm and pulling her away from the makeshift dance floor.

Shoshanna twisted out of his grasp. "What's your problem?"

"I don't want you hanging out with him," Max said forcefully. He lanced Vlad with a look that dared the punk to so much as peep out a hello.

"I'm sick of you telling me what to do!" Shoshanna argued hotly. "Vlad's cool."

"He's trouble."

"You're just jealous because he's smarter than you."

Now officially pissed off, Max yanked Shoshanna's arm free. "Well, if I'm the dumb one in the family, then you must be one retarded bitch."

"What*ever.*" She flipped her hair and started back toward the throng of dancers.

Max stopped her. Gently this time. "Just don't do anything stupid, okay? Drink until you puke up your guts. I don't care about that. But *no drugs.* Do you understand me? That stuff can kill you."

Shoshanna smiled. "Max, you worry too much. Enjoy your party." And now she openly mocked him. "I'll be home before sunup, *Daddy.* You can test my urine then." With that, she disappeared into a colorful sea of gyrating bodies.

Max sighed, made serious eye contact with the blonde he planned to claim later on, and proceeded to do what came naturally with a frosty bottle of Skyy.

He wandered around the rooftop, admiring his handiwork. This party had been seriously low maintenance—some gravel, a few well-placed bars, sound equipment, protective railings, and a dozen or so group-size beds. Of course, finding sheets tough enough to survive stiletto-heel stabs, spilled drinks, and the occasional vomiting incident had been a challenge. But the coverings were holding up well.

For a moment, the view of the Empire State Building

took his breath away. This was the *real* high life—a party on the roof, underneath the stars, in one of the greatest cities in the world.

"This is so glamorous," a Russian-born model, perched on one of the beds like a spoiled poodle, praised to no one in particular. "The fresh air is making me crazy! I feel like getting naked!"

Max smiled. The music was hot. The girls were hotter. And the liquor supply would last until breakfast. Life on Tar Beach was pinch-me-I-must-be-dreaming good.

Nothing could go wrong tonight.

Vanity stood alone in the corner, taking a hit off a rotating vodka bong while Mariah Carey's "We Belong Together" wafted through the New York air.

Here it was, barely midnight, and the DJ had everyone snuggled into slow dances. What a tool. She openly scowled at Cash Boden, the young music controller who had delusions of being the next DJ AM or Mark Ronson. Good luck, wannabe.

Okay, so the boy gave off a pinch of James Dean vibrations. Big freaking deal. Any baby from a family dynasty who says no to politics could claim that much. At the end of the day, Cash Boden was merely *faux* rebel. Translation: Just another rich white boy openly desperate for street cred. Final assessment: Beyond pathetic.

Suddenly, Vanity could feel her face relax as her eyes got that marbles-in-her-head sensation. Oh, yes. Almost drunk. It was a fantastic state of mind.

A greedy hand reached out for the glass water pipe that contained the smoothest vodka Vanity had ever tasted. The hard liquor had been imported from Holland, and the innovative packaging made it go down all the better.

She mourned the bong's escape from her grasp, watching as more party people moved in to sample the unique experience. With a roll of her eyes, she ditched the scene. Bygones. Let them have it.

Vanity needed something else to blast off anyway. After all, she was only *almost drunk,* and she wanted to careen past *officially drunk* and crash right into *completely wasted* territory. Cheap champagne would be the fuel to get her there in a hurry.

She spied a fat green bottle of Korbel on one of the bars and rudely snatched it up, fully intending to drink every drop all by herself.

Vanity pretended to flirt with an older guy who talked a lot of shit about managing a band that she'd never heard of. She allowed him to open the Korbel on her behalf.

The cork popped as loud as a gunshot.

Vanity laughed gleefully, taking off with the bottle and leaving the mystery group manager to wonder if she'd ever return.

Alone with her champagne, Vanity gulped it down, relishing the sweet taste and the oceanic sound of the bubbles. Maybe now she could drown her head out of its perpetual state of self-loathing, regret, and anxiety. Alcohol did a much better job of it than Dr. Parker, which is why Vanity had deep-sixed therapy altogether.

She swept a gaze over the rooftop crowd and noticed Dante and Max standing off to the side, mentally stripping girls with their stares as they whispered back and forth, occasionally punctuating their commentary with naughty laughter.

Vanity chose to countervail her irritation by drinking more. She tipped the Korbel to heaven and guzzled deep. Finally, the liquor began to strain her mind and ripple her vision in a way that gave her the incentive to soft-pedal the intake. But that instinct passed quickly, and she downed even more.

It was easier to be schloggered than to think about the message boards. It was easier to be schloggered than to moon over Dante. And it was easier to be schloggered than to reflect on her questionable future. Basically, no matter the problem, facing it soaked in alcohol was just easier. DJ Wannabe began to pump sounds of life, fading out Mariah and bringing into the mix Annie's "Chewing Gum," a bubblegum confection if ever there was one. But at least the song had a solid beat for dancing.

Not far away, Vanity noticed Christina taking a hit from the vodka bong that would surely go straight to the party lightweight's brain. But she looked great tonight in her embroidered powder blue tunic by Tory Burch, paired with a gauzy white peasant skirt and her signature scuffed cowboy boots. There was a real haunting quality to Christina's beauty.

Vanity zeroed in on it, swaying to Annie's singsong rhythm, tracking the introverted Latina artist with a ray-gun gaze. She gave deep thought to Christina's unrequited crush and the sweetly obsessive devotion that had played itself out in the creation of *Harmony Girl*. At least it proved that *somebody* loved her.

Suddenly, Vanity sensed her breath cut short with an immediate desire. The feeling hit her like a crime of passion, and she vaulted toward it, powered by the strength of the strangely stirring but unavoidable impulse . . . to kiss Christina. She felt wicked for thinking it, for wanting it, but something as strong as an electrical surge propelled her forward.

And there was no turning back.

The shocking moment tore through Christina like a cleaver. From out of nowhere, Vanity was upon her, mouth to mouth, kissing passionately, groping hungrily.

The long-simmering desire surfaced in tandem with

the surprise. It swirled through her insides at such a furious pace that it became a riot of emotions. Leading the charge was an animalistic wanting that thrummed with a dizzying erotic force. Christina wanted this. She wanted it enormously. She wanted it forever.

A delicious heat transferred from Vanity's body to Christina's, and the sensation made her blood bolt, left her starry-eyed, and hooked her like an instantly addictive narcotic. It was her *second* kiss. But from her *first* love. And the psychic pull was mind-melting.

Christina became vaguely aware of their surroundings. The public spectacle of the Sapphic clinch had ignited the crowd, but she tuned out their rowdy cheers and dirty taunts as the kiss thundered on.

"Shit! This is hot!" a guy yelled. "Keep going! Bite her nipple!"

All of a sudden, Vanity drew back, cupped Christina's flushed cheeks in her hands, and cackled loudly. "God, I'm *so* drunk!"

Christina could only stand there speechless, barely managing a sheepish smile as the rest of her tried to get a handle on the situation. Every synapse in her body felt zapped, like a mosquito that had flown into a blue bug light and died instantly.

Vanity patted Christina's cheek and playfully beaked her nose. "You're a good kisser, though. One day you'll make some girl very happy." She chuckled, bent down to reclaim her bottle of Korbel, and tottered away, a vision of gorgeous destruction in her silk tuxedo blouse by Monique Lhuillier and re-mended Tsubi jeans that hung dangerously low enough to reveal her thong.

For Christina, the incident was paralyzing. Just the sight alone of Vanity could make her chest ache. And the sensation of the kiss had awakened a fever and a kind of beauty that was instantly all-consuming. But it was over. As fast as it had started, it was over.

And what was Christina supposed to do now? Dismiss this as some disposable Madonna-Britney moment brought on by alcohol? She couldn't do that. Too many emotions had been stirred up.

The rush of hurt nearly upended her. To escape from the loneliness . . . to act out the secret love that existed so sadly in her heart . . . to do that only for those fleeting seconds . . . oh God, it made every breath that much more painful . . . because now she knew how amazing it could feel . . . how wonderful it could be.

Just in the nick of time, the vodka bong came back around. Christina took another turn, desperate for any elixir that might obliterate her sorrow, help her forget the secret horror that awaited her at Salvation Pointe. The liquor tasted raw and burned going down.

She looked around at all the drunk, happy faces, yearning to be one of them. Why not? This time the internal play-back of her mother's just-say-no drinking lectures couldn't bring the party to a screeching, guilt-ridden stop. Christina was in New York. All she had to do was slur the hotel address to a cabdriver or stumble back to the building on her own.

There was no danger in drinking the pain away. Not here, not tonight.

"What the hell was *that?*" Dante demanded.

Vanity stared back at him, completely saturated by al-cohol, holding up the Korbel bottle like a shield. "I'm just having some fun," she sneered.

"How could you do that to Chris—"

"I'm putting on a show, dickhead! Isn't that what everybody wants? I figure they're sick of watching the same thing over and over again on the Internet, so I busted out with a live version. Whoo-hoo!" She twirled around, nearly toppling over.

Dante stopped her fall and tried to take the cham-pagne, but Vanity yanked it from his reach with such force that she lost her grip on the bottle.

"Look what you made me do!" Vanity shrieked, look-ing down at the broken green glass as if it were a shattered dream.

"Let's go back to the hotel," Dante said quietly. "I think—"

She silenced him with a nasty look. The rage in her eyes looked like ammunition that had been stockpiling for months. "What do you *think*, Dante? Tell me. I'm dying to hear it."

"I think you've had enough."

"And I think I'm just getting started," Vanity shot back. She started off toward the bar.

Dante reached for her hand to stop her.

Vanity snatched it away as if his touch could burn. "Leave me alone!"

Dante backed off, raising both hands in a show of surrender. "Fine. Get even drunker. I don't give a shit anymore."

"Anymore?" Vanity asked incredulously. "That seems to imply that at some point you *did* give a shit."

For Dante, this moment crystallized all the reasons why he didn't want to be here—on this trip, at this party, in this argument. Vanity was the worst kind of drunk girl. Liquor brought out her demons and gave her stamina. She could fight all night if the mood struck her.

"So when was it, Dante?" she demanded. "Just for the record, when did you care?"

He stood there in silence, knowing that whatever he said would get twisted around in Vanity's Korbel-soaked mind. So he offered nothing.

"Yeah, that's what I thought."

Dante watched her leave, wracked with guilt, indecision, and exhaustion. The impulse to follow her was there. But he resisted. His thing with Vanity was complicated. Christ, maybe it was *too* complicated.

As Vanity walked out, a pretty girl walked in. She had tousled hair. She wore too much makeup. She seemed oblivious to the fact that one of her tits was about to spring loose from her top. The wasted smile on her face conveyed a vacant simplicity. She looked easy on all levels.

No personal dragons.

No public scandals.

No asshole father.

Tomorrow he would deal with the difficult girl. But tonight he wanted easy. Grabbing a beer, Dante walked over to say hello.

From: Max

U r missing out, slave girl. Tar Beach is outta control.
Ditch your rich bf and hop a plane.

11:57 pm 4/08/06

chapter fifteen

ax Biaggi launched the shoulder-cannon missle straight into the unmarked mini-van, taking out a terrorist sleeper cell in one perfectly choreographed explosion.

"Do you perform your own stunts?" Pippa asked, mesmerized by *Hijack II* on the forty-two-inch plasma screen.

They were wheels up, the only passengers on a luxurious Boeing 737, destination still unknown.

"As much as I can get away with," he answered from the enormous swivel seat upholstered in beige leather. "I'll try anything. Love the adrenaline rush. But sometimes studio suits step in to hold me back. They get tight-assed about insurance riders."

The movie recaptured Pippa's attention. The star was

shirtless now, his defined chest rippling, powerful arms corded with muscle, six-pack abdominals as defined as the underside of a turtle. Every part of him was larger than life on the screen, digitized to a level of such pixel-perfect clarity that she could actually see the beads of sweat on his brow, count the lashes that swept a shadow over his eyes, and make out the tiny scar just under his lower lip.

Max Biaggi chuckled. "I worked out with a trainer for six months. All for this one scene."

Pippa gave him an appreciative gaze. "It seems to have stuck."

He raised an eyebrow, zapped off his action hero image with the remote, and stood up. "Less that. More you." Taking her hand, he pulled Pippa to her feet. "I haven't kissed you yet, Star Baby. Do you want me to kiss you?"

"Yes." The breath shuddered from her lungs as she answered. His face was so close. She could smell the wonderful masculine scent of him. Oh God, this is why he was a movie star. The magic worked on the big screen. The magic was working right now, too. On her.

Bit by bit, Pippa's desire was unshackling, even as a vague sense of danger began to build. Why was she suddenly afraid? Perhaps it was her own lust frightening her. She wanted him to do things that no boy or man had ever done to her before . . . or would again. It stopped here with Max Biaggi. Tonight. And for the rest of her life.

Pippa's heart stood still as her lips moved in to claim Max's mouth.

But he didn't just pull back. He recoiled from her.

Confused, Pippa leaned forward. "Aren't you going to kiss me?"

The expression on his face was certain, his tone matter-of-fact. "Of course not. I don't kiss whores."

Pippa backed away from the cruel rebuke, the unexpected words hanging in the balance of the horrible, surreal moment. This had to be a trick of the mind. "Wh-what?" She barely managed to speak.

He gave her a quizzical look. "I thought you knew." Now his voice was hard. "You're a whore, Star Baby. I only kiss wives and girlfriends. But that doesn't mean we can't have a good time." He grabbed her arm, pulling her roughly toward the front of the plane.

Pippa tried to resist, but his physical strength proved too much. Dragging her to the private stateroom, he pushed her onto the bed.

This couldn't be happening. But in Max Biaggi's once devoted eyes she now saw a monster. Pippa felt sick. A hot tear rolled down her cheek. "Turn the plane around," she said in a small voice. "I don't want to be here anymore."

There was a predatory gleam in his stare. "Too bad. I own you, Star Baby."

"I'm not for sale," Pippa shot back, surprised by the strength and defiance in her tone.

He laughed at her. "Every whore has a price. Vinnie charged me top dollar for you, and I expect to get my money's worth."

Pippa lay there on the expensive Frette sheets, suspended in a state of hyperreality as the ugly truth blistered and burned.

Vinnie had sold her out.

Max Biaggi had bought her dirt cheap.

Pippa closed her eyes, steeling herself to remember the moment, that beautiful, innocent, hopeful moment, when she believed a girl like her could actually have the best of everything.

"You can keep your shoes on. I'm done with that part of your body." And then he unfastened his belt.

Coldplay's "Speed of Sound" lilted from the speakers as Max surveyed the scene. Again. In fact, he couldn't stop admiring it. Tar Beach, his first event outside of Miami, would go down as a certified smash.

His latest social creation was an exquisite body crush of tipsy models, Hollywood actors, young professionals, X-factor teens, and assorted scene makers.

Dante sidled up, guzzling a beer, bobbing his head to Chris Martin's ivory key rhythm. He hooked an arm around Max's shoulder.

Together they watched a fine-ass WB starlet in stiletto heels struggle to stand up on one of the beds. She spilled her drink. She giggled. She twirled her shiny purse in the air.

"Girls can say whatever they want about me," Max began, feeling philosophical with the rise of his blood-alcohol level. "They can say I'm a dick, that I never call—"

"That you cry like a little bitch after you come," Dante cut in.

"Okay, that happened once," Max joked back, not missing a beat. "But I was drunk, and our family dog had just died. It was a vulnerable time."

Dante laughed.

"You should go find Vanity," Max said. His voice dropped an octave. He was serious.

"Oh, I should?" Dante asked, his tone punchy.

"She's going through a rough time."

"Vanity's the kind of girl who will *always* be going through a rough time."

"This is great, man. It's spring break, and you've got my oldest friend feeling like shit."

"Sorry. Maybe she can get together with all the girls you've screwed over. I hear there's a meeting at Madison Square Garden."

"Fuck you," Max said. And he really meant it.

"Right back at you." Dante pushed his half-empty Miller Light into Max's hand. "I'm out. You give good party, dude. But I'm over it."

Max watched him go, part of him wanting to chuck the bottle at Dante's retreating back, another part wanting to run after the asshole and talk things out. In the end, Max just stood there as a helpless feeling washed over him.

The fabulous five clique was imploding. Pippa had bailed on spring break altogether. Vanity had come along only because Max practically held her at gunpoint until she said yes. Dante didn't give a shit about anyone but himself. And poor Christina had reluctantly joined the trip, only to be broadsided by one of Vanity's manic drunk slut episodes. Great friends. Good times. Whatever.

Max tried to forget about the dysfunctional group. If the others chose to wallow in misery, then let them. He planned to party up. It was one in the morning, and Tar Beach was shifting from wild to more wild.

He spotted the lissome blonde who'd been on his dick radar since she arrived. Disposing of Dante's drink, he made his way over. "You're hot." As an approach line, this never failed. After all, what girl didn't want to hear it?

"So are you." She smiled, giving a little flip of her flawlessly blown-out hair. "I'm Bethany. I work in the fashion industry."

He grinned at the vague career mention. She probably fetched Starbucks and picked up dry cleaning for some bitch editor at *Vogue*. "I'm Max. I pulled this event together."

"Wow," Bethany murmured. "Hats off to you."

Max shrugged. "I'd prefer panties off, but we're still getting to know each other, I guess."

Bethany beamed back a sexy look. "Uh . . . we might get there eventually."

He stepped closer, just as the DJ pumped up the volume with LL Cool J's "Rock the Bells." The old-school classic made him itchy to dance. But right now he was itching more for Bethany. "I should probably be up front with you about something."

She looked at him expectantly.

"I'm only interested in you for sex. And by that I mean sex right now and not tomorrow or next week. Don't give me your cell number, because I won't use it. Don't ask for mine, because I won't tell you what it is. I'll want you to give me head, but don't expect the favor returned unless you get frequent waxes. I prefer the Brazilian. And I hope you do yoga. My new favorite position requires a girl to be limber."

Bethany laughed. "Well . . . at least you're honest."

Max nodded. "I figure girls are tired of party talk bullshit from guys. My new motto is to keep it real."

"Actually, it's sort of refreshing," Bethany said.

"So do you want to go back to my hotel?"

Before she could answer, there was a commotion in the center of an impromptu dance throng that arrested Max's attention.

What he saw next stopped him cold, making the pounding hip-hop beat sound as hollow as voodoo drums. Everything shifted to slow motion.

Shoshanna lay flat on the gravel, her body convulsing in a violent seizure.

Max raced toward her, desperately knocking out of the way anyone in his path. "Sho!" He cried out her name into the New York night.

Finally, he reached her, the fear inside him total, his guts knotted. Never before had he seen a face so white. Shoshanna's cheeks were bloodless. She looked almost translucent.

Max glanced up, scanning the area until he found Vlad Singer. "What did you give her?" he demanded.

"Nothing!" Vlad insisted. But as his voice told the lie, his nervous eyes revealed the truth.

"Somebody call nine-one-one!" Max screamed. And then he lunged for Vlad, grabbing two fistfuls of fabric on the punk's hoodie and shaking hard. "What did you give my sister, man? Tell me!"

"N-n-nothing," Vlad stammered. "I-I . . . d-don't know what happened."

A primal urge flooded through Max's body, filling him with a propensity for violence so strong that it scared the hell out of him. Vlad Singer was the smartest guy on the roof but suddenly wanted to play dumb as a cow. And Max could kill him for it. Right here. Right now.

"Oh my God!" a female voice shrieked.

Max spun around to see an ashen-faced Bethany standing over Shoshanna's now listless body.

"She's not breathing."

The music drowned out Bethany's voice, but Max could still read her lips. The gears in his brain jammed. He didn't know what to do. He wouldn't know how to cope.

And "Rock the Bells" played on.

The cruel joke was on Christina. But even more cruel was the fact that she wouldn't mind if Vanity played it on her again. That's how amazing the kiss had felt.

Christina had been to parties before where two girls put on a show of fake kisses to drive a guy crazy. The encounter with Vanity was altogether different, though.

Vanity's kiss had been *real*. A hot, deep soul kiss full of hungry lips, wet, probing tongue, and curious fingers running up and down Christina's body.

Even now, a few hours and God knows how many drinks later, Christina's mind still hummed from the sensual memory . . . the smoothness of Vanity's cheek against hers, the erotic way Vanity's hands had played with her hair, the instant patch of wetness the attendant arousal had brought to Christina's panties.

But the most devastating aspect of all was the force of Vanity's kiss, the sheer deliberateness of it. Vanity knew how to throw down, going after Christina's mouth with such confidence, passion, and intensity. It was like one of those big romantic movie kisses. The hero finally decides that he can't live without the heroine, the music swells, and he unleashes a kiss that literally takes her breath away.

But it was all just a joke. Vanity was doing it for the audience, not for Christina. A hot tear accompanied the harsh reality. God, her emotions were all over the place. She was really beginning to feel the steady intake of 3. The vodka had a carb count of zero. That made it diet friendly. The company was owned by Jermaine Dupri and Janet Jackson. That made it cool.

With the popular vodka bong long gone, Christina had sought out the 3 shots as the next best thing. They were served up in the kind of tiny paper cups that nurses used to dispense pills to patients. How appropriate. Because the liquor definitely had medicinal properties. Right now she was feeling no pain.

All of a sudden, the rooftop visuals began to blur and spin around. Christina stumbled, falling into a passing partygoer.

"Hey, easy, girl," the guy said with a wink, reaching out with both hands to steady her. He looked like an Abercrombie ad come to life—rich, handsome, and chiseled in the manner of an Ivy League star athlete. "You okay?"

"I'm fine," Christina shouted, fighting to be heard above the music.

"Correction—you're shit-faced. If I was a jerk, I'd take full advantage." Then he laughed and walked off.

Christina teetered away, clumsily negotiating past a protective railing, seeking refuge closer to the ledge. She balanced her hands on the concrete. It felt cool and rough to the touch as she peered down.

Nine floors below, a line snaked outside the building. Fashionable late-night social animals waited to be admitted into the elevator and whisked to the top. She watched curiously as expensive cars pulled up, discharging more of the same.

On the street, Christina noticed a gaggle of Japanese girls bunched into a tight huddle and snapping digital pictures of themselves. From way up here, one of them looked exactly like Keiko.

As the realization hit, Christina continued to stare. They were partying on the street. They were partying on the roof. They were partying all around her. She wondered if this is what it felt like to be invisible.

Even Christina's friends took little notice of her. Vanity had slipped away, no doubt to some bigger, better VIP event. Dante had stalked out in a huff, spotting her in his peripheral vision and offering barely so much as a wave good-bye. And Max was somewhere chatting up his next conquest.

People said that New York was the loneliest city in the world, that it was an island filled with millions of people in a race against time to pursue their own agendas. Walking shoulder to shoulder on the busy streets, they stared straight through you, if any eye contact took place at all.

Christina could feel it right now. The dull ache of isolation. And the deeper sting of irony. Here she was, on a spring break excursion with friends, part of the fabulous five, in with a popular group, a set of circumstances that she never dreamed would be possible, and yet Christina had never felt more alone. She really was the invisible girl.

To Vanity, Max, Dante, and Pippa, she was so clearly the interloper, the disposable one. To Keiko, she was just a sacrificial lamb for a political con. And to her own mother, she was nothing more than a public image liability.

Oh, yes. *The conservative Senate hopeful with the lesbian high school daughter.* It was a label that now followed Paulina Perez everywhere. And on those rare occasions when she actually looked Christina directly in the eyes, her mother's disappointment, shame, and regret was painfully transparent.

Three little words crept into Christina's fuzzy, vodka-soaked consciousness. It was a turn of phrase. It was a state of mind. But it was also an answer to her misery, an escape from the hell that would be Salvation Pointe: "Better off dead."

She struggled to hoist herself up and onto the narrow ledge. Once there she weaved side to side, back and forth, swaying as she fought to secure her balance and gaze at the streets below.

Manhattan mocked her. The city seemed glittery, powerful, and full of exuberant life. In stark contrast, Christina felt dark, weak, and empty of all hope for happiness.

The wind picked up the hem of her skirt. Goose flesh sprouted on her bare thighs as the cool breeze slapped against them. She stole a downward glance, wondering if the impact of skull and bone on concrete would hurt. But then nothing could hurt more than the inner demons tormenting her now.

Behind her, the music carried a strange echo. It sounded weird inside her head. Suddenly, she sensed a disturbance. Somewhere in the dim fog of her drunken mind she heard Max screaming his sister's name.

Christina turned to look back. As she shifted her feet for a better sight angle, one of her boots got tangled up in a left-over string of Christmas lights. Attempting to shake it free, she stumbled. It was just enough to lose her balance.

At the last possible moment, she scrambled, desperately trying to fall in the direction of life.

Back toward Tar Beach.

Back toward *Harmony Girl.*

Back toward Max.

After all, what if he needed her help? Christina wanted to be there for him. She wanted to be there for her future, too.

Would she be accepted into the Savannah College of Art and Design? And if so, what about the brilliant career that would follow?

But then came a terrible cold panic as her feet slipped from the safety of the ledge. Because all of a sudden she knew that she wouldn't be.

It was so strange. Moments into the fall, the sadness miraculously left her heart. Peace at last. She didn't even scream going down. All she did was play back her mother's cruel words from that cruel day.

I would rather you commit suicide than live that life.

For Dante, it was a long walk back to the hotel. Not in physical distance, but rather the time of emotional reflection. Hard facts were hard facts. He was a premium-grade asshole.

Trying to compare Max's general attitude toward girls to his treatment of Vanity had been a pathetic sign of weakness. The truth was, Dante needed to come clean on his own shit.

Punishing Vanity for the deal-shark methods of her father was simply a case of Dante being a passive-aggressive jerk. She didn't deserve any of the blame for *his* idea of sampling Henry Mancini's "Le Jazz Hot" turning up as the hook on Speed Freak's hit single. Simon St. John and Juan Barba were the true guilty ones.

Still deep in thought, Dante paced the area outside the Court, the boutique W Hotel tucked inside the Murray Hill neighborhood. Max had booked everyone here because of the reasonable walking distance to the building that would host Tar Beach. It was a sixteen-story hotel but maintained the cozy feeling of a hideaway.

Dante had never stayed in a room more posh—sleek modern furniture, large-screen TV, plush bedding, a terry-lined bathrobe, and a minibar to cream over. Dante had wolfed down the thirteen-dollar peanuts just for the fuck of it.

Of course, for Max and Vanity, and to a lesser degree Christina, the bling lifestyle was merely business as usual. Having a "whatever, whenever" button on their hotel phones, which gave them twenty-four-hour access to anything in the city, was simply no big deal.

Dante tried Vanity's cell. No answer. The girl could be anywhere. But he had a feeling she was upstairs in her room, crashed for the night. And so he marched inside the Court, through the almost-deserted lobby lounge, and straight to the elevator. There were things Dante needed to say. There were things Vanity needed to hear. The doors couldn't open fast enough. He was anxious to find her before losing his nerve.

Dante mulled over his future in real terms. Hopes for a serious education past MACPA were bleak, and every statistic was stacked against guys like him. According to the sociologists who crunched the numbers, Dante was likely to earn less than half of a college graduate, three times more likely to be unemployed, more likely to commit a crime, and also more likely to develop a substance abuse problem.

He laughed out loud at the bitter forecast. Shit, it was either that or *cry*. Okay, on paper, Dante Medina was no girl's Prince William. But so what? There was one stat in Dante's favor. And it was in Vanity's favor, too. He was more likely to love her better than anyone else.

The elevator stopped on the eleventh floor.

Dante raced to Vanity's suite, his heart expanding with each urgent step, his body tingling with excitement. Yes, this was one of those half-drunk, late-night epiphanies. But it was real, too. No more games. No more replacement girls. This time he would put in the work to make it last. Dante and Vanity. They were *meant* to be together.

When he reached her room, Dante was shocked to discover that the door was ajar.

He knocked three times. "Vanity?"

Silence.

A strange foreboding came over him. Instinctively, he knew that something was wrong. He pushed open the door and stepped inside.

The room had been trashed—furniture turned over, throw pillows, coffee table books, and other decorative accents strewn about, curtains ripped from the rods. A sudden fear hit him like a punch in the chest.

He called the front desk for security and searched for answers until someone arrived. On the bed he found Vanity's purse with all of her belongings intact, including cash, credit cards, driver's license, and Sidekick II. Just as he was about to look inside the bathroom, he heard approaching footsteps.

Two hotel staffers appeared in the open doorway, an assistant manager and a security guard. They seemed unfazed by the condition of the room, listening impassively as Dante relayed his discovery.

The manager commandeered the phone, placing several calls and speaking in a hushed tone while the guard burdened Dante with a series of routine questions that were leading nowhere fast.

"Your friend was refused service at Wetbar a short time ago," the manager announced, referring to the hotel's smoked-glass nightspot that overlooked Lexington Avenue. "She was intoxicated and didn't take the news well." He gestured to the destruction around the room. "Apparently, she decided to act out her displeasure here."

Dante tried to wrap his mind around the idea of Vanity trashing her own room. But it didn't add up. He shook his head. "She didn't do this."

"Have you been drinking, too, sir?" the manager asked with an arched brow.

"I've had a few beers, but that doesn't mean I can't recognize a break-in when I see one," Dante snapped, narrowing his eyes. "What's your excuse?"

In answer, the manager traded a weary look with the security guard.

Dante fought to remain calm. Neither one of these jizzbags gave a shit. He thought about calling the NYPD, then decided against it, figuring he'd only get the runaround from them, too. No more time could be wasted.

"This isn't some stupid drunk girl drama, man!" Dante cried. "Something happened here. Something *bad.*"

"The hotel staff is on alert," the manager tried to assure him. "I'm sure your friend is still on the property, and—"

Dante waved him off. "Don't even finish." He felt a sudden, impossible thirst and glanced around for a bottled water. Nothing. Snatching an empty glass, he stormed into the bathroom and flicked on the light. And then he froze.

Smeared in red across the mirror were the words "A DIRTY BITCH WUZ HERE."

Dante moved closer, reaching up to touch the defaced glass with his index finger. What he discovered next scared him stone-cold sober.

The message was written in blood.

To be continued . . .

MTV Books
proudly presents

a
*fast girls,
hot boys*
novel

beautiful disaster
kylie adams

Coming soon in trade paperback from MTV Books

Turn the page for a sneak preview of
Beautiful Disaster

Slowly, Vanity came up from the deep, unconsciousness lifting like a fog. She experienced the vague sensation of being alert. And then a wave of nausea hit. Worse than any hangover.

Her body lurched violently. On reflex, she attempted to cover her mouth with her hand. But the movement met with painful resistance.

Oh God! Both arms were manacled to the bed frame with thick rope that burned her wrists when she tugged for freedom. Her feet were tied down, too. She was spread-eagled. Immobilized. Vulnerable. Defenseless.

Shock, fear, and confusion overrode her physical urge to vomit. Terror ruled, leeching the heat from her body.

She began to shiver and fought to reclaim the memory of the lost hours.

Where was she? How long had she been here? Who had done this? What was going to happen to her?

Vanity worked herself into such a state of distress that a film of sweat slicked her from head to toe. Tears rolled down her cheeks. Why couldn't she remember?

She screamed. And not just any scream. It was a wail of horror, despair, and frustration—a plea for release, a begging for mercy.

Suddenly, she heard music. Loud music. The thrash-metal assault drowned out her cries and ramped up her fears.

Megadeth's "Symphony of Destruction." The song choice was a dead giveaway. Vanity's heart pounded in a stutter beat as one thing became clear. Who had done this to her.

It was no longer a question. Because now she knew the answer.

Look for
Beautiful Disaster
wherever books are sold.
Coming soon in trade paperback
from MTV Books

Dear Readers,

I hope you enjoyed *Bling Addiction,* the second book in my new FAST GIRLS, HOT BOYS miniseries. The first installment, *Cruel Summer,* ended with a number of situations unresolved. Did you go insane waiting to find out what happened? Well, "Oops . . . I Did It Again!" I've left you hanging on a cliff with Vanity, Dante, Max, Pippa, and Christina in more suspended states of peril and uncertainty. But don't despair. All the questions in your mind will be answered in the next book, *Beautiful Disaster.* Including the *big* reveal. Which one of the fabulous five meets an early death? You will *definitely* find out!

My first goal is to write fun books that take you on a wild, page-turning trip. But the characters in this series are young and facing a host of complex issues, many of them dealing with sexuality. There's a great line by the journalist

Ariel Levy on the subject of teenagers and sex. In her book *Female Chauvinist Pigs: Women and the Rise of Raunch Culture,* she writes, "Sex is different from drugs; we can't tell them to just say no and leave it at that. Sexuality isn't something they can opt out of."

It's no secret that we're living in a culture that provokes teenagers to act out in adult ways like never before. Yet at the same time, $1 *billion* has been spent on abstinence education since the late nineties. A major paradox. And the characters in FAST GIRLS, HOT BOYS are trying to navigate that minefield, often with disastrous results!

In a world where Paris Hilton is celebrated, I think a lot of girls will identify with Vanity and Pippa, who put a great deal of energy into their looks, trying to appear as enticing to boys as possible. The end result is that they get attention—some positive, some negative—but little of it has anything to do with what's happening inside them.

Then there's Christina, an introverted girl on a painful journey of confusion and shame regarding her sexual orientation. The guys in the story aren't off the hook, either. Dante might have the physical moves, but emotionally, he's as clumsy as a colt. And Max, no matter his vast experience with many willing girls, is still a seventeen-year-old guy afraid to ask the embarrassing questions.

Basically, the fabulous five—like so many of America's youth—are occasional victims of sex *mis*education. This problem goes beyond what *isn't* happening in schools. It also encompasses what *is* happening on the Internet. Sex is Topic A when teenagers go online to seek health advice and information, but with millions of sources resulting from a Google search, much of the content on deck is likely to be false. Sometimes dangerously false. Dina Borzekowski is a media and adolescent health specialist at Johns Hopkins University, and she recently recommended these websites as resources teens could trust for accurate information and thoughtful guidance:

www.youngwomenshealth.org
www.teenhealthfx.com
www.sexetc.org

Okay, relax now. This very special school counselor moment is over! But I had to impart what little wisdom I've garnered in the course of researching these books.

If you can't get enough of FAST GIRLS, HOT BOYS, then visit my official website at www.readkylie.com for free reader extras. There's an exclusive three-part short story called "Jailbait," which is a prequel focusing on Max's not-so-baby sister, Shoshanna, the ultimate wild child. She's fifteen going on twenty-one. The first chapter was posted with the release of *Cruel Summer,* and the second chapter is available now. I hope you enjoy "Jailbait."

The second extra is a free Podcast available for immediate download on iTunes. This multisegment radio show is packed with a few spoilers on *Beautiful Disaster,* cool information about Miami, plus dish on the latest fashion and trends. Just log on to iTunes and type FAST GIRLS, HOT BOYS into the Podcast search engine. At no charge you can download the program and subscribe to future Podcasts. There's also a *Bling Addiction* iMix available on iTunes. Just log on and type BLING ADDICTION into the iMix search engine. You'll see a fun playlist featuring songs and artists mentioned in the book. This is part two of the soundtrack to the lives of Vanity, Dante, Max, Pippa, and Christina.

Wait—there's more! On my website, take a moment to join the K-List, otherwise known as "Kylie's Inner Circle." There's a special sign-up tab for fans of FAST GIRLS, HOT BOYS. I'll be sending out periodic e-mails on the miniseries, future writing projects, and site updates. And don't forget to post me a K-mail. I love hearing from readers, and I'm dying to know what you think about *Bling Addiction*!

With all good wishes,

Kylie Adams
www.readkylie.com

P.S. Go to my website and take the "Die Young, Stay Pretty" poll. It's your chance to vote on which character you believe will meet the tragic end in the FAST GIRLS, HOT BOYS series. Is it Vanity, Dante, Max, Pippa, or Christina? Cast your vote now. And find out what other readers are thinking, too!

Your attitude. Your style.
MTV Books:
Totally your type.

Cruel Summer

First in the *Fast Girls, Hot Boys* series!

Kylie Adams

Life is a popularity contest...and someone is about to lose. In sexy Miami Beach, five friends are wrapping up high school—but one of them won't make it to graduation alive....

The Pursuit of Happiness
Tara Altebrando

Declare your independence....After her mother dies and her boyfriend cheats on her, Betsy picks up the pieces of her devastated life and finds remarkable strength and unexpected passion.

Life as a Poser

First in the *310* series!

Beth Killian

Sometimes you have to fake it to make it....Eva spends an intoxicating summer in glamorous Hollywood with her famous talent agent aunt in this witty, pop culture-savvy novel, first in a new series.

Plan B
Jenny O'Connell

Plan A didn't know about him....When her movie-star half brother—a total teen heartthrob—comes to town, one very practical girl's plans for graduation and beyond are blown out of the water.

Printed in the United States
By Bookmasters